MARGARET - THE BIG BEAUTIFUL BRIDE

FROM BRAVE NURSES TO COURAGEOUS BRIDES

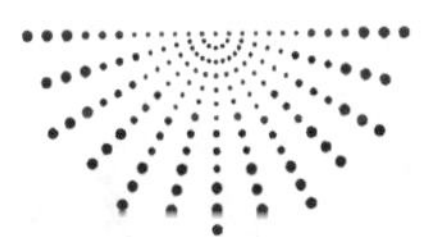

INDIANA WAKE

SWEETBOOKHUB.COM

FROM BRAVE NURSES TO COURAGEOUS BRIDES

Welcome to this new series of three books for you my wonderful readers.

Each of these books is a complete story, with the journey of the three of them running through the whole series. The three friends were nurses who worked on the battlefields from 1861 to 1865. After the war, they found themselves lost and with little future.

They take a chance to head west to find love and a new life but things don't all go as they had hoped.

Will they find happiness, love, and all they dreamed of, or have they found a worse life than the one they left?

Read on for Margaret's Story.

Books in the series:

Carolyn – The Orphaned Bride

Margaret – The Big Beautiful Bride

Leticia – The Grieving Bride

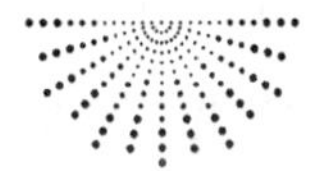

Carolyn sniffed in the sweet sickly scent of the bouquet of daisies in her hand. She stifled a smile by biting her lower lip. Sherman had a habit of surprising her with little gestures like this. It was a great reminder of why she fell in love with him in the first place. He brought her flowers, took her on long walks, and constantly reminded her of how beautiful and important she was to him. Sometimes, when Carolyn was alone with Sherman, it felt like a dream. He was good to her. Too good.

"Are you sure you're all right?" Sherman asked. She could feel his eyes studying her face. "How's work? Are you stressed?"

Carolyn sighed and shook her head. "I'm all right, Sherman. Thank you for asking. We had a lot of customers today, but we're already used to the crowd... I guess."

Getting her a job at Wendy's, the popular, small restaurant in Appleton was Sherman's doing; everyone loved him and he had helped her to get the position. Thankfully, he had been taken on as the preacher. Appleton was a small farming community, they had been here just two months after arriving in South Dakota.

It didn't take long before the townsfolk warmed up to Sherman. They had been in need of a preacher and he fell into the position and was much loved. Carolyn, Margaret, and Leticia all worked at Wendy's in exchange for a place to stay and a small wage.

Working at Wendy's was different. Carolyn smiled, the good kind of different. No one made silly or rude remarks about them, and pretty much everyone they met had been friendly.

"How about you? Are you all right?" she asked in return.

Sherman nodded. "I am, thank you. I just thought to drop by and say hello before I head to the church. Seeing your sweet smile makes my day. I'll come by again tomorrow."

"It's always nice to see you. Thank you for the flowers, again. They are beautiful," Carolyn said with a smile. "You're so thoughtful."

"I'm glad you like them." Sherman briefly ran a finger across her cheek. "See you later, Carolyn."

"See you." Carolyn was breathless from the tender touch.

Carolyn waved at Sherman as he strolled down the road. He occasionally glanced back at her, checking to see if she was still watching. In the short time they had spent together, Carolyn could brag that she knew virtually everything there was to know about him. He was a simple man, with an inspirational and intriguing past. On numerous occasions, Carolyn would daydream about holding deep conversations with Sherman while they were seated on the ground, by the lake, staring at the reflection of the sun in the still water. She was doing it again, as she watched him disappear around the corner.

"Are you going to keep gawking at Sherman, or are you going to help us clean up so we can go to bed?" Margaret asked, standing with one hand on her ample hip.

Carolyn rolled her eyes. "All right, I'll help," she whined. "Sherman's gone anyway so there's nothing to stare at."

Carolyn set the bouquet of wildflowers down on the counter and picked up a broom instead. The evening rush always left the restaurant pretty messy and cleaning up after everyone left took a lot of time. Hence, Carolyn, Margaret, and Leticia had learned to use that time to discuss their day. Once they got back to their room, they lay down on their beds and went straight to sleep. It had become a routine for them.

"I can't lie, seeing you and the preacher together makes me feel warm inside," Leticia said as she wiped down a table. "It feels like... scattered pieces coming together perfectly. The feeling you get when you put that last piece of the puzzle in."

Carolyn squinted her eyes. "You make it sound so complicated."

"I do?" Leticia asked, her eyes widening.

Margaret shrugged her shoulders. "I get it. She means you're both made for each other, Carolyn. Your relationship with Sherman feels... comfortable."

"Comfortable?" Carolyn questioned. "Oh, to me it is exciting...."

Leticia groaned in frustration. "Would you stop reading the wrong meaning into this and accept the compliment? You and the preacher look really good together. I still don't understand why it's taking so long for you to get married."

"Oh, it's only a matter of time now, Letty," Margaret said. "Soon, Sherman is going to drop on one knee and ask for Carolyn's hand in marriage. You'll see."

"Well, I sure hope so," Leticia said. "Carolyn's prospects seem the most promising and I would hate to see them crumble given what we have been through at the hands of Porter Hathaway."

"Oh, please don't even say that man's name," Margaret begged. "The thought of him nauseates me."

"I agree." Carolyn shuddered. "I'd like to think less of that man and more of our future without him."

"Sorry," Leticia shrugged. "However, Carolyn, do tell us." A grin crossed her face and her eye shone with expectation. "Are there any signs that Sherman might be in possession of a ring? One he plans to propose to you with? You both have been courting for a while now."

Carolyn set the broom down and began to rearrange the chairs. "Well – I cannot say for sure, but he has been dropping subtle hints on that particular subject." The grin that spread across her face was contagious.

"Subtle hints?" Leticia was grinning too. "Tell us more, what do you mean by subtle hints?"

"Letty, you're obviously not blind," Margaret retorted. "You've seen how he constantly brings her flowers, talks to her before he makes a decision, buys us things, and takes Carolyn on walks. Sherman has his eyes set on only Carolyn. Surely, he wants a future with her."

"Right. But there should be more. I want it so much." Leticia was chuckling now and her two friends chuckled with her.

"You're impatient, how must Carolyn feel?" Margaret said.

"I'm enjoying things as they are," Carolyn said. "Who doesn't like to be spoiled?"

"Yes, but a proposal," Leticia said. "But what do you want, Carolyn? If Sherman were to propose, let's say, tomorrow. Would you say yes?"

"In a heartbeat," Carolyn said. "I truly want to spend the rest of my days with him, and deep down, I want to believe that a union with him is well on the horizon, but..."

"But what?" Margaret and Leticia chorused.

"What's holding you back, Carolyn?" Margaret asked softly.

Leticia scoffed. "Don't tell me it's us. You know very well that we would support whatever it is that you do."

"No, I know. It's not about that." Carolyn paused and sighed. "I just wonder if I am up to the task of being a preacher's wife. I mean, Sherman has a lot of responsibilities on his shoulders. People trust and look up to him. What if I am not enough?"

"What do you mean?" Margaret asked. "It's you, Carolyn. If you aren't up to the task, who is?"

"Maggie, you know what we have been through. A lot has happened to us in such a short time. We still have not fully recovered from all that happened in Minnesota."

"Minnesota is behind us," Leticia said. "If you keep dwelling on the past, how do you expect to move forward? It's like you said, we need to start thinking of our future."

"We worked at a saloon, Letty," Carolyn said. "Not just any saloon, the infamous Porter Hathaway's saloon. Thankfully, we were able to escape from that horror house with our dignity and sanity, but that doesn't change the fact that we are considered saloon girls. Or we were. What if this fact comes to light and people misunderstand the entire situation? What if people find out, and it, in turn, damages Sherman's reputation? One he is working so hard to build? That's what I'm worried about. That's the reason I don't think I am up to the task. I love him too much to do that to him. Not after all he has done for us."

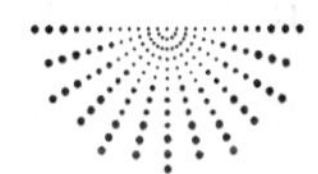

CHAPTER TWO

*L*eticia and Margaret exchanged looks and dropped their heads avoiding her gaze. That cut Carolyn to the bone. It appeared that deep down, they knew her worries were valid. They knew that her past, their past, however unwanted, might damage Sherman's reputation.

Carolyn slumped onto a chair and shut her eyes. To think that she had come so far, escaped so much, but that happiness still eluded her... it was too much.

"Truthfully, I worry about that too," Leticia said softly. "I mean, we know what we went through to get to where we are now. We're the only ones who know how terrifying it was. We've made acquaintances, and people actually like us here in Appleton. It scares me that our reputation could be ruined in a heartbeat if people find out we were Porter Hathaway's saloon girls."

"Stop, stop it!" Margaret lifted one hand up. "Both of you. Stop with the sudden depressing tone. Those days are behind us. Far behind us. It's been months now, and while we are still trying to get over the ordeal, I strongly believe that we shouldn't hold back and should just go for what we want at this point. What has happened, has happened and there is no changing that. We cannot keep dwelling on it. Please, let's move on."

Leticia rolled her eyes and took her seat too. "You've always been the optimist, haven't you, Maggie?"

"We all need to be optimistic at this point," Margaret explained. "We deserve to be happy and we will be. I believe it, and you should too. I'm going to get a happy ending."

Leticia smirked as she rapped her fingers on the wooden table. "Is this about Edwin? The happy ending you so crave?"

"Oh, it's most definitely about Edwin." Carolyn giggled. "You want him to be your happy ending, don't you, Maggie?"

Margaret crashed onto a chair too, the cleaning up forgotten as she sighed deeply. "Fine. Yes. It's about Edwin."

Leticia clapped. "I knew it."

"He's the one good thing that has happened to me after everything we've been through," Margaret explained. "If I'm being honest, I want a future with him. I want what Carolyn has with Sherman."

"Well, from what we have seen, Edwin really likes you too," Carolyn said. "I don't think you have much to worry about. He knows everything there is to know about you, and he is comfortable with it."

"That's the thing. Sometimes, it doesn't seem like he is comfortable."

Leticia tilted her head to the side. "What do you mean?"

"How do I put this?" Margaret clicked her tongue. "He tends to shy away from conversations about us, what we're doing, any plans for a possible future... that sort of thing just gets avoided. Sometimes, he seems scared, other times, it's like he's sitting on the fence. But then again there are times when it seems like we're on the same page. It's all so confusing."

Carolyn placed her hand on the back of Margaret's palm. "Give it time. It's still too early to be worrying about this. If Edwin is unsure, let him figure it out. You can see in his eyes that he dotes on you. Don't go worrying yourself about it."

"At least, not yet," Leticia added. "Don't worry about it."

Margaret sighed and nodded. "All right then. I'm probably overthinking it. I just worry if he is... well, if it is my... my size."

"Stop it, you are beautiful and there is nothing wrong with you," Leticia said.

"You are not so big," Carolyn said. "Not at all."

Margaret tried to smile but she still remembered the potential husband, Gregory King, whom she had been introduced to. She remembered the look of disgust on the man's face as he rejected her for being fat.

"Oh, I see," Leticia said. "You are thinking about that awful man... something King.... Remember, Porter had paid him to reject you. It was nothing to do with you."

"I know... but I worry."

"Don't, you and Edwin will be fine. I bet your size has never crossed his mind, everyone can see that he is smitten with you," Carolyn said. "We will all be fine... I hope. Now, can we finish up and go to bed? We still have to get up pretty early in the morning, and I am exhausted."

Leticia rose to her feet. "Yes, please."

Carolyn was in dire need of Margaret's normal optimism but she hated to see her friend worried. At least, she knew Margaret had nothing to worry about, but, the more she thought about her relationship with Sherman, the more convinced she was that he was better off without her in his life.

Carolyn cared for Sherman so much that she was ready to stay away from him if it meant protecting his reputation. But on the other hand, she yearned for Sherman's company every minute of the day and she hated being apart from him. No matter how much Margaret and Leticia tried to convince her that the bad things were behind them, Carolyn couldn't shake off the feeling that they weren't. She was still haunted by her past, and it was affecting decisions in her present. It was affecting her happiness.

"We'll be fine, Carolyn," she whispered to herself. "We have to be."

* * *

Edwin Grant stood outside the church. He groaned and shut his eyes. They were sore, heavy. Staring into the sun was a bad decision, given that he had a raging headache that refused to go away.

Rubbing a hand through his light brown hair he leaned against the fence. Sooner or later, he had to do something about the constant headaches. He had also lost a bit of weight, which bothered him because he was already a lanky man. But with the workload that he had at the church and the constant worrying, the sudden loss wasn't surprising. Still, these headaches were becoming a cause for concern.

"Uh, I think I need to lie down," Edwin whispered to himself as a wave of dizziness seemed to roll over him. He had barely gotten any sleep the night before.

Months ago, when they first arrived in Appleton, Edwin had held high hopes that the new town was going to be better for him. He had always thought that the environment in Minnesota was the reason he was always so fatigued. That was why he was quick to jump at the idea of a fresh start somewhere far from there with Sherman.

He loved the church, and he highly respected Sherman, so it wasn't a difficult decision.

However, it didn't seem like the new place was any better than Minnesota. Edwin was around good people that he could call family, and he loved everything about the community. But the fatigue and constant worrying hadn't stopped. There were days when he would wake up and be too exhausted to get out of bed. He had no idea what was causing him to feel this way, but he knew he had to figure it out.

"Hello, Edwin. How are you?"

The sound of a lady's voice startled Edwin. He lifted his head and stepped back, his heart hammering against his chest.

CHAPTER THREE

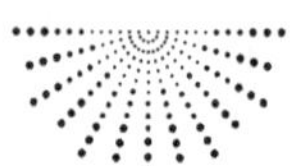

$\mathcal{E}$dwin did his best to hide his shock, it was another part of his illness. Was it an illness to be so tired and yet at times wired? Shaking his head he pushed his own feelings away and concentrated on the present. "Good morning, Carolyn," he managed with a weak smile.

Carolyn studied his face for a couple of seconds. "Good morning, Edwin. You look... exhausted. Is everything all right?"

Edwin slowly nodded. "Everything's fine. Thank you for asking. How are you? And how's work at the restaurant? Sherman said you are all doing so well there."

Carolyn laughed awkwardly. "Sherman? I would have thought that you'd hear it from Margaret. You are very close, or so I believed?"

Edwin blushed a little at her teasing. He and Carolyn had little to talk about. Whenever they happened to cross paths, they typically exchanged greetings, talking about the church, Sherman, or Margaret.

"I did hear it from Margaret too." Edwin nodded. "But I was aware from the start that Sherman was helping the three of you look for work."

"We love working at the restaurant. So far, it has been amazing, and there's no reason to complain. It can be tiring, but... well, we love it."

"I'm pleased. It's good that you like the work you're doing." Edwin smiled and felt it was a little more genuine. "What brings you to the church today?"

"I'm here to see Sherman. We're taking a walk together."

"Oh, that's nice to know."

"Edwin, is everything really all right?"

Edwin lifted his head to meet her gaze. It was the third time Carolyn had asked him that question and she had a worried look on her face. What was it that she was sensing?

"What?" Edwin said softly. "What do you mean?"

"I'm asking if everything is all right with you."

Edwin inhaled deeply and slowly started to nod. "Everything's perfect, Carolyn. Thankfully, the town is very welcoming, and the church is really working hard to do some good in this community. Especially Sherman. He has made his way into the hearts of the local farmers too. The women you included who came here with us are all safe. It's a pretty peaceful place. I like it."

Carolyn fiddled with her skirts and sighed. "That's all true. It's a pretty peaceful town... but you know that's not what I'm talking about."

Edwin squinted his eyes and brought both hands to his hips. Perhaps, if he acted obliviously, Carolyn would not keep pushing him on the issue. This was not something he was ready to share and yet... she had a way of finding things out. "I'm sorry, I don't seem to understand what you're driving at," he said with a shrug that he hoped was pretty nonchalant.

Carolyn threw both hands in the air. "Edwin, we started working at the restaurant weeks ago. You came once, with the members of the church for lunch, and you haven't been there since. I'm just going to say it." She took in a deep breath. "I really thought that you wanted more with Margaret. It seemed obvious. But now I'm unsure. That's why I'm asking if everything is all right. You haven't come to the restaurant to visit Margaret, or talk to her alone." She waved her hands at him and paused.

What did she want in return? He cared for Margaret but he could hardly tell Carolyn that he had been so tired.

"Your attitude worries me because it worries Margaret. She really cares about you, but it doesn't seem like you care as much about her. Plus, you don't look too well, Edwin, that's also why I think something is wrong. If you don't want to talk to me, you can talk to Margaret at least. I'm only concerned for Margaret's happiness. She's been through a lot, and I would hate to see her sad again. So, what I'm saying is that I think you both need to talk."

Carolyn's voice was slowly starting to sound like it had an echo. His shoulders felt heavier than usual like there was a weight on them, and he was fighting hard to keep his head upright. Edwin glanced at a chair just by the entrance to the church and imagined himself sitting on it. But it would be rude to walk away from Carolyn without giving her a response.

"Everything's fine, Carolyn," Edwin said. "We've both just been busy, that's all. I'm fine."

"But, Edwin…"

"I said I'm fine," Edwin knew his voice was raised, sounding slightly irritated. He sighed and rolled his eyes. "I told you everything is fine. Please, leave it be."

His harsh tone caused Carolyn to take two steps back. She cleared her throat uncomfortably and diverted her gaze. Even as the words flew from his mouth, Edwin knew that he was overreacting. But he was too tired to think straight.

"Edwin."

Sherman's voice pulled their attention. Edwin stepped back as Sherman approached them. From the look on his face, it was obvious that Sherman had heard his outburst.

"Good morning, Sherman," Carolyn greeted him. "Edwin and I were just having a chat."

"I heard," Sherman said to Carolyn but with his eyes boring into Edwin. "What was that, Edwin? Please watch your tone when speaking to a lady. There was no reason for your demeanor or such a harsh tone."

Edwin ran his hand roughly across his face. "I know," he said. "Carolyn, I am so sorry. I... lately, I've been feeling..."

"It's all right," Carolyn said. "I was prying. I'm sorry."

Edwin shook his head lazily. "No, you don't have to apologize. It's my fault. I'm sorry."

"Carolyn, would you give me a minute? I'd like to have a word with Edwin."

Carolyn turned to Sherman. "Of course. I'll wait for you here."

Nothing was going well for Edwin that morning. In addition to the headache and fatigue he woke up with, he was going to spend the rest of the day feeling guilty for his behavior. Nothing was working.

Edwin followed Sherman and they stopped at the foot of the staircase. "Sherman, I apologize. I didn't mean to lose my temper like that. I don't know what got into me."

"I get that," Sherman said. "And I know you, Edwin, that's why I'm surprised. If I'm being honest, I've also noticed that something is not quite right with you. Something's changed, and that worries me. Are you going to lose your temper too, if I ask you what it is that's bothering you?"

"Sherman, I'm so sorry," Edwin said closing his eyes as a ray of sunshine seemed to be knifing into his skull.

"Did you and Margaret quarrel in any way?" Sherman asked. "When we first decided to move from Minnesota, you were one of the first parishioners and friends that decided to help me. Then you met Margaret, and that was the happiest I had ever seen you. Lately, you seem to have taken a step back. May I ask why?"

"I've been constantly tired of late," Edwin explained. "I'm guessing that's the reason I've been so irritable. I'm a bit tired, that's all."

"Is that it? You just need rest?"

"I just need rest," Edwin answered.

Sherman nodded. "All right then. Get some rest, Edwin. I don't want to see you roaming around the church today. I need you to go back to the boarding house, get into your bed, and remain there until tomorrow morning."

Edwin chuckled lightly. "Noted. Thank you, Sherman. And please, apologize again to Carolyn for me. I was out of my mind. I'm sorry."

Sherman placed both hands on Edwin's shoulders and tapped him lightly. "It's all right. I'm sure Carolyn understands. I want you to take a step back from your church duties too. I think you're taking on too much. That's what's stressing you. And make matters right with Margaret too. You might not want to admit it, but something is off between the two of you. Whatever it is, make it right."

"I will. See you tomorrow. Have a nice stroll."

"Thank you."

Edwin watched Sherman return to Carolyn's side with a faint smile on his face. He turned around and headed into the church, his mind set on Sherman's words. He wanted to do right by him, and Edwin hated that he had given Carolyn such an unfavorable impression, he had almost shouted at her and that would not do. Perhaps, taking a step back from all the work he had in the church was the best idea. At least until he was able to gather his strength.

Sherman and Carolyn were right. Edwin knew that his relationship with Margaret had changed over the last month. He had barely talked to her in recent weeks. There were times when he would go to the restaurant, but he would stop at the door and retreat. They were right to worry.

He would go lie down, rest and then he would feel better, but as he started to turn, he suddenly grew light-headed. Edwin grabbed the arm of the pew and shut his eyes tightly as his vision blurred.

Still, the room spun and blackness overwhelmed him. There was no air and he struggled to breathe. Then his legs began to buckle and there was nothing. Edwin fell to the cold, hard floor between the pews.

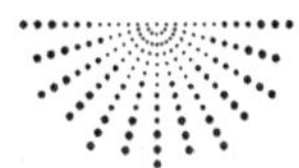

CHAPTER FOUR

"I wanted to tell you something yesterday but you were already asleep when I got back."

Margaret had woken up that morning to Carolyn's soft voice calling out to her. Once she opened her eyes and met Carolyn's gaze, Margaret sensed what it was about. She knew that Carolyn was visiting Sherman at the church yesterday, and had hoped that she would run into Edwin. Her friends had a habit of looking out for her, even when she claimed that she was all right. It was no surprise that Carolyn took it upon herself to confront Edwin about their relationship.

Margaret sat up and rubbed her eyes. "You saw Edwin yesterday?" Margaret felt hope surge in her chest but the look on Carolyn's face pushed it away.

Carolyn nodded. "Yes. He was a little distant, strange... I say strange 'cos Edwin isn't usually like that."

"What happened? Did he say something?"

"He looked tired," Carolyn started. "I went to the church to spend the day with Sherman. We were supposed to meet in the yard, so while I waited for Sherman, I ran into Edwin. We got talking, and I asked if he was all right. I kept insisting that he talk to me because it seemed like something was wrong, but he got angry and... irritated."

Margaret arched her eyebrows. "Angry?"

"Yes. His tone was stern and he asked me to stop asking him questions. He even rolled his eyes at me."

"What?" Margaret scoffed. "Edwin? Edwin rolled his eyes at you?"

Carolyn nodded in response. "I was shocked myself," she added. "It's not like him."

Margaret found it hard to believe. The Edwin she knew would never lose his temper, especially not with Carolyn. Edwin had a constant smile on his face. In fact, Margaret had never seen him frown. His laugh was contagious, and he told silly jokes that were so absurd, that they made her laugh. Margaret found it strange that he got annoyed when Carolyn was only concerned for him. It didn't make any sense.

"He apologized immediately," Carolyn said. "I could see that he regretted his outburst too. I don't know. Something tells me he wasn't particularly angry at me. He seemed frustrated. I just triggered him with my questions. I felt so terrible."

Margaret exhaled calmly. "Well, at least now, I'm sure something is going on. Why would Edwin be like that?"

"Sherman thinks he is taking on too much work at the church, that's why he's exhausted."

Margaret shook her head. "You really think that's what it is? Edwin has never complained about anything like that before."

"Well, perhaps it's taking a toll on him. You can never tell, Maggie."

"The fact still remains that something is going on with him and I need to see him. It bothers me." Margaret tried to smile but the feeling inside her was one of dread.

Carolyn placed a hand on her back. "I know. Are you going to see him today?"

"I am." Margaret nodded. "I'll ask Penny for the afternoon off and head to his boarding house. I think that's the right thing to do."

"All right then. Don't worry too much. If Edwin is merely tired like he says he is, then Leticia and I were right. All he needs is time to get back on his feet. Just be there for him as much as you can."

"I will. Thank you."

As they prepared for the day, Margaret's head was spinning with ideas on how she could make Edwin feel better. She had thought that he was staying away from her because he had lost interest in their relationship, but apparently, that wasn't the case. At least, that was what she had to believe.

"A picnic sounds like a lovely idea," Margaret said as she tied her bright red hair into a ponytail. "Edwin loves to spend time outdoors. He'll like the idea."

With that, Margaret spent all morning making a picnic lunch basket. A break was what Edwin needed, and she wanted to be the person that gave it to him. Edwin was good to everyone. He was friendly, and he treated people with respect. That was the reason she took his curt tone towards Carolyn as a sign that something was wrong. On top of that, they had to talk. It had been a while since they sat down to have a decent conversation.

Margaret stared at the lunch basket on the table that she had spent hours making. She sighed and nodded. "This should suffice."

"Are you on your way to the boarding house?" Leticia asked Margaret from behind the counter. "To see Edwin?"

"I am," Margaret answered. "We're having a picnic."

Leticia smiled. "That's good. Carolyn and I will cover for you, so go and have fun."

Margaret gave Leticia a big thank you smile. She picked up the basket and headed to the boarding house in the mild afternoon sun. Appleton was a farmer's community, hence most of the paths were bordered by lines of trees and crops, fenced with wood and barbwire. Margaret would playfully wave at the cows and goats as she walked by some of the farms. So far, Appleton was the best place she had lived; even though it had only been for a short time, she felt at home here, relaxed, ready to start a new life. She wanted nothing to change.

Calm yourself, Maggie. He still likes you. Margaret said to herself as she made her way to Edwin's house. Only, it was not easy. She really cared for this man and yet, something told her that things had changed, was it over?

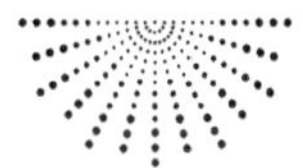

aggie stood outside Edwin's door. Her courage had left her and she wondered if this was the wrong thing to do. Was it too forward? Was it pushy? Maybe, she should just leave him alone and let him come to her if he wanted to see her?

All these thoughts raced through her mind as she tried to muster up the courage to knock. It had been a while since they last spoke to each other, hence she had no idea what his reaction was going to be. Pushing all her worries aside, Margaret rapped her knuckles on the door and quickly stepped back.

As she heard the door unlock, she held her breath.

"Maggie," Edwin beamed.

His watery smile was the same, but it wasn't fooling her. There were dark circles around his beautiful, honey-brown eyes that she constantly loved to stare into. His rosy lips were slightly chapped, and his chiseled jawline seemed even leaner. Like he had lost some weight.

"Good afternoon, Edwin."

"Good afternoon, Maggie."

Edwin reached for her hand and brought it to his lips. He planted a kiss on the back of her palm like he always liked to do whenever they met. It felt like things were back to normal between them. He had the same cheerful look, and yet, there was something a little drained about it.

"I take it you spoke to Carolyn." Edwin, lowered his head, breaking eye contact. "That's why you're here."

Margaret slowly nodded. "I did."

Edwin let out a heavy sigh. He stroked the back of her palm gently while still avoiding her gaze. "That wasn't me. It was, but... I didn't mean to be so..."

"It's all right, Edwin. Carolyn understands. In fact, she thinks it's her fault for asking you too many questions, not knowing that you simply needed to rest. I understand too. It has been rough for all of us since we arrived in South Dakota. It's fine to take a step back sometimes to gather oneself. Carolyn said to tell you that it's been forgotten. It's fine. I'm just glad to see you smiling again."

Edwin's smile got even brighter. He lifted his head and met her gaze. "Thank you, Maggie."

"You're welcome," she responded. "Would you like to share a meal with me? I'd like us to have a picnic this afternoon. That is… if you're up for it."

"A picnic?" Edwin asked. "At our favorite place?"

"Yes," Margaret answered, almost in a whisper.

"I'd like that," he answered. "I'd like that very much."

A feeling of relief washed over Margaret. Edwin took a few minutes to tidy himself, when he was done, he took her hand and they made their way to the small meadow. She placed her palm on her cheek and gently patted it, hoping that she wasn't blushing hard. Somehow, she had forgotten what she had been worried about in the first place. Edwin was himself again, and she hoped it remained that way.

When they arrived at the meadow, Edwin spread the blanket under a tree. Then they both sat, and stared into the silent space. There was only the tweeting and chirping of birds, and a cool breeze to keep them company. Margaret constantly glanced at Edwin, hoping that he said something, but he stared at his fingers instead.

"Wendy's is the best place I have ever worked," Margaret started. "I mean, no offense to Union Field hospital. But I'd prefer working in a place where I don't have to wonder if that day was my last."

Edwin chuckled lightly. "That's understandable."

"Penny named the place after her dead grandmother. She said she learned all the recipes she knows from her nana, and uses them at the restaurant. It's pretty sweet."

Edwin nodded slightly but was he listening?

"Penny is really understandable too. She praises us, talks to us, and treats us really well. The regular customers at the restaurant are lovely too. And really friendly. Most of them attend church, so we see them almost all the time. How have you been, Edwin? Did anything fun happen to you in the last few weeks?"

Edwin lifted his head. "No," he said.

"Oh. Well, all right…"

Margaret glanced at Edwin and began to fiddle with her fingers. Things had gotten awkward quickly. Edwin was awfully quiet and his smile had dwindled. Perhaps she should not have pushed him to come on the picnic. Maybe he still needed to rest. Or maybe there was more to it. Panic squeezed her heart and sent a chill down her arms.

Staying calm, Margaret placed a hand on Edwin's shoulders and met his eyes. "Edwin, are you truly just tired, or is there something else going on? You know you can tell me anything."

Edwin's eyes were watery all of a sudden. His eyebrows twitched as he parted his lips to speak. But then he looked away, drew in a deep breath, and feigned a smile.

"I'm all right, Maggie," he said with a quivering voice. "I promise. I know I've been a terrible person to you these past few weeks, and I have you doubting my intentions towards you, but I promise I will make matters right between us soon. Trust me."

There was sincerity in his eyes. Margaret saw it, but instead of it bringing her relief, it worried her. "I trust you," was all she managed to say.

"Thank you," he answered, facing her fully, with a smile that seemed forced on his face. "So, the town dance is around the corner. The people at the church have been talking about it all week and it sounds like it's going to be all shades of fun. Would you please go to the dance with me, Maggie?"

Margaret giggled. "I would love to, Edwin. Of course, I'll go with you," she said. "But I have to confess that I am not the most graceful dancer. I can't count the number of times I've tripped and fallen while trying to dance."

Edwin threw his head back in laughter. "Well, that makes two of us. I am an awful dancer. We would make the perfect match."

Margaret laughed too as his statement put her at ease, but deep down she knew she wasn't exaggerating. Her legs always fought each other every time she tried to dance. Edwin had asked her so sweetly, that she had to find a way to not embarrass him.

She closed her eyes slightly, imagining what the night would be like when she felt Edwin's warm palm cup her cheek. Margaret lifted her gaze and instantly held her breath as Edwin leaned in. He touched her cheek with his other hand, and once he was close enough that

Margaret could feel his hot breath on her skin, she shut her eyes.

His lips met hers in a chaste, sweet kiss. Heat rose from her belly, filling her chest and flaring in her throat as Edwin pulled his lips from hers and pressed his forehead to hers. They remained that way for almost a minute while he stroked her cheek with his thumb. It was magical and filled her with joy and a feeling that all was right with the world. This was where she was meant to be, this was her future. Then Edwin pulled away and leaned on the tree, interlocking his fingers with Margaret's.

"Tell me something about yourself," Margaret spoke first, in a bid to fill the silence. "We always talk about me. Tell me about you."

Edwin clicked his tongue. "Let's see... what's there to know?"

"How'd you meet Sherman? What were you doing before you started working in the church? I've only heard about your experiences working in the church, but we haven't talked about what you did before."

"Well, there's not much to know," Edwin started. "I was orphaned at the age of twelve. I had to live in an orphanage. I lived there for a year, and I couldn't do it anymore. It was restricting and suffocating, the people were hard, cold, and cruel. So, I fled. I left the orphanage and was something of an aimless drifter for a long time. That was until I came in contact with Sherman. He helped me find a purpose."

"That must have been so difficult, you were so young. I'm glad he found you," Margaret said. "I'm happy you found a friend, and you found your path in life."

Edwin turned to her and squeezed her hand gently. "I'm glad I found you," he said softly, causing tingles to run down her spine.

Maybe she had worried about nothing for his sweet words and sweet moves filled her with joy and hope, but there was something she couldn't put her finger on. Something was wrong.

CHAPTER SIX

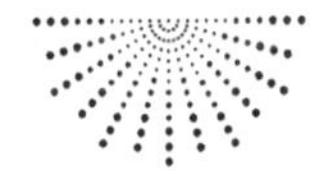

*T*he same dream again.

Leticia picked up the knife from the kitchen table and placed the carrot on the cutting board. Chopping the vegetables for the soup was a task she ought to have completed the day before, but she put it off until the morning. She had to hurry, it was almost time for the lunch rush.

Things had been going smoothly since they arrived in Appleton. At least, that was what she thought up until last week when she began to have the same dream over and over again. Leticia had thought that she had made progress. She had not thought about Dwight in a long time, hence the depressing thoughts were kept at bay.

But then it started again. The dream she used to complain about back in New Hampshire. Dwight appeared to her, and she remembered all the good times they had together. Then, it would turn into a nightmare. She would see him dead once more, and be jolted awake. It was depressing, and as much as she tried to hide it, she couldn't.

If only there was a way to get rid of the nightmares without involving Carolyn and Margaret. The last thing she wanted was to worry them or make it seem like she was overreacting. All she wanted was to think of Dwight without feeling like a knife had been thrust into her heart, or like the weight of the world was on her shoulders. She wanted to think of Dwight and smile at all the happy memories they had together.

"Ah!" Leticia shrieked in pain and flung the knife away. She pressed her index finger with her right hand, restricting the blood from flowing too fast.

Margaret dropped the spoon in her hand and rushed over to Leticia's side. "What is it? What happened?"

Carolyn appeared too through the backdoor. "Leticia, I heard you scream."

"I cut myself." Leticia pulled her other hand away and revealed the dripping appendage. "I was chopping the carrots and I got distracted."

Margaret gasped. "That is a lot of blood, Leticia. How deep did you cut it?"

Carolyn stepped forward and took Leticia's hand. "Let me see."

The cut was deep. Leticia didn't need to see it to know. She bit her lower lip. It was a sharp, stabbing pain, but she could bear it. What she was more concerned about was how she was going to explain what distracted her to Carolyn and Margaret.

"This needs stitching," Carolyn said. "And cleaning. We don't want it getting infected. We need to clean it, disinfect it and patch it up."

"We can't do that, Carolyn," Margaret told her.

"You can, Maggie," Leticia said. "I just need this patched up and I'll be fine. We're nurses. It's a piece of cake."

"Nurses that haven't practiced in a while," Margaret said. "Plus, we don't have the tools to use or any form of disinfectant here. We need a doctor."

Carolyn nodded. "Maggie's right. I'll wrap this up for you, and we'll take you to the local doctor. His name is Oliver Randall. He attends the church too."

"Carolyn, I'll take her. I know the local doctor too," Margaret said. "One of us needs to stay back for the lunch rush, and also explain to Penny."

"All right, I'll hold down the fort while you're both gone," Carolyn said, examining the injury. "It hurts, doesn't it? Sorry, Leticia."

Leticia shrugged her shoulders. "Oh, it's my fault anyway for being distracted while I worked. I'll have this patched up and I'll be back, don't you worry."

Carolyn nodded. She quickly wrapped Leticia's finger in a piece of cloth to stop the bleeding. When she was done, Leticia left the restaurant with Margaret. They hurried down the road, making their way to the center of the town. Leticia had heard of the local doctor too, but she had never seen the man.

"Oh, it's still bleeding," Margaret noted. "It shouldn't be bleeding so much. We need to hurry."

They arrived at the doctor's clinic after a few minutes of walking. Margaret knocked on the door and waited impatiently for the doctor to answer. When the door creaked open, Leticia lifted her head.

"Good morning, Doctor Randall," Margaret greeted. "I'm Margaret Sampson. This is Leticia Baker. We had an accident in the kitchen. Leticia cut her finger pretty badly while trying to chop a carrot."

Leticia slightly tilted her head to the side, instinctively assessing the man. He was a tall middle-aged man with broad shoulders. He greeted them with a smile that revealed a perfect set of white teeth. The local doctor was handsome. Leticia had to admit. The man had silver streaks in his light brown hair, and his eyes were icy blue. A familiar color of blue...

"Those eyes..." she mumbled.

"Please, come on in," Oliver said.

Leticia shook her head to snap herself out of her thoughts. She had a terrible habit of examining people she met for the first time and making mental notes about them.

"Please sit here, Miss Leticia," Oliver said to her, gesturing to the high stool in the center of the room.

"Thank you," Leticia said. "And please, call me Leticia."

"Only if you call me Oliver," he answered, retreating. "I've seen the both of you at the church a couple of times, and also at the restaurant where I regularly have lunch. Please feel comfortable."

Leticia adjusted in her seat and cleared her throat. The pain hadn't subsided, but she felt more at ease. She always tried to stay away from hurting herself because it frustrated her, hence putting her in a bad mood. But right now she didn't feel frustrated, this man had a way of calming her. There was no need to beat herself up about an accident.

"Let me see..." Oliver mumbled, reaching for Leticia's finger.

Leticia mildly quivered when Oliver touched her hand. In that split second, a stream of current had coursed through her and caused her to shiver. Oliver peered at the injury, slowly twisting her finger to get a good look at it. His touch was gentle and attentive. Leticia felt safe and yet excited.

"It's a pretty deep cut, but it's nothing for you to worry about," Oliver explained. "I'll clean the wound and stitch it."

Leticia nodded and braced herself for it. Oliver walked around the room, gathering his tools into a small tray while Margaret remained by Leticia's side. He returned shortly and got to work.

After about a minute of silence, Oliver cleared his throat, "I should say that I see how hard you women work at Wendy's. Every time I visit, there is always a crowd and the three of you are rushing around the room, catering to everyone so efficiently. It's impressive, Wendy's has never run so well."

Margaret smiled. "Thank you, Doctor Randall. I'm the one always attending to your table because you always sit in the same spot."

"I do," Oliver said. "I really like that spot by the window."

"I noticed." Margaret smiled.

"You came with the church. With the preacher and his parishioners?" Oliver asked, facing Leticia.

"We did actually," Margaret answered in her stead. Feeling a touch of color hit her cheeks. They had said that the women rescued from the saloon were parishioners and had never mentioned the way they made their living in the past. It was not something she wanted to talk about in case the truth got out.

"Well, I'm happy that the preacher and his congregation are here in town and fitting in so well. We were very short of the gentler touch and they... you... have all become such an asset. Sherman has done a lot of good work here in the short time since he arrived."

Leticia let out a sudden sharp gasp and jerked. She cleared her throat awkwardly as she lowered her gaze.

"Leticia, what's the matter? Why did you gasp?" Margaret asked with a concerned look on her face.

Leticia glanced at Oliver who was staring at her too, worry written all over him.

"Nothing," she stammered.

"Are you sure?" Oliver asked. "Apologies if I was a little rough, stitching can be worse than the original injury but it is necessary. However, if you feel pain anywhere else, please let me know."

She shook her head vigorously. "No, sorry... I'm fine, Doctor. I don't feel any pain. Well, only in my finger, but I'm fine."

Oliver paused for a second and although Leticia's head was bowed, she sensed that he was watching her.

"All done," Oliver said a few minutes later, taking a step back. "I will give you something for the pain, but you have to come back in a few days, Leticia. I need to check the wound and see if it's healing properly. So please, do come back."

Nodding, she jumped off the stool. "I will, Doctor. Thank you very much," she said, scurrying to the door.

"Wait, I haven't given you the medicine yet," Oliver said, stopping her in her tracks. "Give me a second."

Leticia didn't have a second. She was fighting really hard to hold the tears that were welling up in her eyes. The pain had transferred from her finger to her chest and it felt like she was suffocating. She thought she was past the worst of it, but apparently, she was not.

"Here," Oliver said, handing Leticia a small bottle. "Take one a day. And remember, come back in a few days."

"I will, thank you, Doctor."

Without giving Oliver a chance to respond, Leticia hurried out of the clinic, staggering into the street.

"Leticia" Margaret yelled after her. "Leticia, wait! What happened?"

Leticia kept walking, without looking back. She needed to get to someplace private before breaking down. No one had to see her like this.

Margaret ran up to Leticia and blocked her path.

"Leticia," she said sternly. "What on Earth threw you off your balance this way? Talk to me. Now. You're scaring me."

Leticia locked eyes with Margaret and with quivering lips, she whispered. "Dwight."

"Dwight?"

"Yes," Leticia whispered again with tears rolling down her cheeks. "I thought I was over it, Maggie. I thought I had moved on from Dwight's death. I thought I was strong, but I cannot seem to handle it. I don't know what's happening."

Margaret's eyes watered too. "Oh, Leticia."

"The doctor had his eyes, Maggie," Leticia sobbed. "Those big blue eyes. It reminded me so much of Dwight and coupled with the dreams, I felt just like a knife had been thrust into my heart. Why can't I just be happy? Dwight is the only man I have ever loved, but this is torture."

Without any further questions, Margaret pulled Leticia in for a hug. She rocked back and forth as Leticia sobbed in her arms. Leticia couldn't help but wonder why it all was happening again. She had lived through that familiar pain before and she thought she was over it. But no, she was mourning the love of her life all over again.

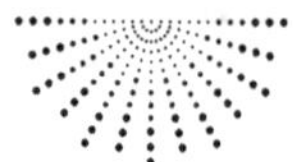

"Edwin, I thought I told you not to come back to the church until you were well-rested?"

Edwin nodded but if he spent one more day inside his room, he was going to lose his mind. Sherman was doing him a favor by insisting that he took more days off, but Edwin wasn't the sort of person who could do nothing all day. Not when everyone else was working.

"I am well-rested," he said, sitting in one of the pews. "I'm fine."

"You just tripped on the steps when you were walking into the church," Sherman said.

"Everyone trips sometimes." Edwin shrugged.

"Right. I still think you should go home. Take advantage of your time off and rest."

Edwin hadn't told anyone about the incident that happened right after he spoke to Carolyn and Sherman. He had fainted for a couple of minutes. He had passed out in the empty pew. Thankfully, no one had seen him and when he woke up, he felt much better. Still, fatigue wasn't a good explanation for it.

"All right, fine. I'll go straight home," Edwin told Sherman. "But I want to visit Maggie first at the restaurant. We don't spend time together like we used to."

Sherman gave Edwin a knowing look. "And whose fault is that?"

"Mine," Edwin stated. "But I'll fix it."

"Good. Are you excited about the town dance that's coming up?" Sherman asked. "Do you think you'll be able to come?"

"Of course. I feel better already," Edwin answered. "In fact, I'm taking Maggie to the dance. It's going to be a night to remember."

Sherman scoffed. "It would be... if only you could dance." He chuckled. "You're not a very good dancer, Edwin."

"I'm not that terrible, am I?" Edwin asked.

"Yes, you are."

"No, I'm not."

"Yes, you –"

"It doesn't matter," Edwin said, cutting Sherman off. "I'll practice some steps before the dance, to make sure I don't embarrass Maggie. She deserves a dance that she'd remember and I plan to give her that."

Sherman placed a hand on Edwin's shoulders. "You really care about her, don't you?"

Edwin nodded. "I do."

"Good. So, take care of yourself, Edwin. Please. I don't want to pressure you into saying anything, but you don't look well. Get some sleep."

How was he going to explain to Sherman that he got adequate amounts of sleep every night, hence he couldn't explain the tired look in his eyes? He was constantly tired, but it wasn't from lack of sleep.

"I will. Stop worrying about me. I don't like it when you worry," Edwin said. "You have a lot on your plate, and I want to be a helper, not a burden. I'll sort everything out, and if there's anything wrong, I'll tell you. Don't worry."

"I'll always worry. You're my friend, Edwin. But I'll trust you too. If there's anything wrong, tell me, all right?"

"All right."

Sherman patted Edwin on the shoulder and walked away. It warmed Edwin's heart to see that he had people around him that cared so much about him and were attentive to every change that occurred in his life, but he hated to burden people. The sooner he got back to his old self, the better.

Shaking off the feeling, Edwin rose to his feet. Thanks to Sherman, his workload had been lightened and the only thing on his to-do list for the day was practicing his dance steps in preparation for the town dance. But his body and his mind were working at different paces.

Edwin took a step forward and his vision got blurry the next second. He staggered back, clutching onto the pillar at the corner of the pew. He had learned to focus on his breathing whenever he had these out-of-the-blue dizzy spells. It kept him stable until the spinning stopped.

"Oh, Lord," Edwin groaned, slowly opening his eyes. It took a couple of seconds for his sight to return to normal, and when it did, Edwin sat back down.

"What is this?" he muttered, it was really starting to worry him.

It was time to face the reality of his situation. Something was happening to him, and he had not a clue what it was. If the dizzy spells, the fatigue, or the fainting continued, then it would be impossible to go to the town dance without risking an incident. He needed to find a solution. Fast.

"I'm not disappointing Margaret again," he whispered, rising to his feet.

The local doctor was the only one that could shed some light on Edwin's situation. So, he made his way to Oliver's place. There were still a few days before the dance and if he got treated before then, he wouldn't have to worry about ruining the night for Margaret. All he had to do was keep the visit to the doctor a secret, for he did not wish them to worry even more.

Edwin stood at the door after he knocked, as he awaited a response. He threw a furtive glance over his shoulder to the path behind him. No one from the church was around, good.

"Hello, good morning."

Edwin turned back around and was surprised to see a young woman standing in the doorway. She looked like the female version of the doctor, with the same blue eyes and light brown hair.

Edwin took a step back to crosscheck the house. "Oh, hello. I, uh... I'm looking for Doctor Randall."

"You're in the right place," the lady said with a smile. "I'm Doctor Samantha Randall, Doctor Randall's daughter."

Edwin stretched his hand towards her. "Nice to meet you, Samantha. My name is Edwin Grant. I work at the local church."

Samantha took his hand and shook it. "Likewise. Please, call me Sam. My father is out making house calls, so I'm here filling in for him. Please, come in."

Samantha looked and sounded like a doctor. She had a bold aura, and she spoke so eloquently for someone so young. But Edwin didn't know her, and he wasn't sure he wanted to confide in a stranger. What should he do?

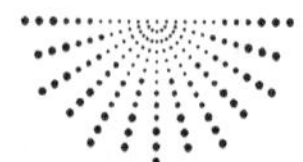

CHAPTER EIGHT

"Oh, I'll just come back when the doctor is in," Edwin stuttered.

Samantha squinted her eyes and tilted her head to the side. "I can assure you that I am more than capable of helping you. My father taught me well. In fact, I've been learning from him for as long as I can remember. I also studied and practiced medicine based on my own merits. You can trust me, Mr. Edwin."

"It's just Edwin," he said. "I wouldn't want to bother you. I can just come back."

"I insist, Edwin," Samantha said, squinting her eyes as she stared straight at him. "At least let me give you a quick examination, Edwin."

Perhaps, she could already tell that something was wrong with him. Samantha had spent the last few minutes studying his face. It made Edwin uneasy. His biggest fear was discovering that he was seriously sick.

He scratched the back of his head. Many men would not think well of a female doctor but that was not him. His reticence was not because of her gender but more because he... maybe, it was fear, he didn't want to know.... "You know what? I –"

"Come in, Edwin," Samantha insisted, standing aside.

A part of him was screaming run away, he didn't want to know. But then, he thought of Margaret. It would be unfair of him to not try and figure out if something was wrong with him. The other part of him was also curious to know what was going on.

"All right then," Edwin said with a sigh. "Thank you."

Edwin walked past Samantha and took his seat on the stool. The room was warm, and strangely homey for a place he was nervous to visit.

"Now, Edwin," Samantha said, taking a seat in front of him. "What brings you to the doctor today?"

Edwin cleared his throat. "Well, Doctor. I came here today because of the dizzy spells I've been having. As I said, I work at the church, so I have a lot of responsibilities. You see, we just settled down here in Appleton, and there's a lot to do. So, when I started feeling tired all the time, I thought that it was all the work I had been assigned. But then, Sherman gave me days off and he lightened my workload. That didn't change anything. I'm still tired all the time, and my head aches. I fainted once, and I get dizzy spells at least once a day."

Samantha scribbled something on a pad and then lifted her head. "These headaches, how often do you get them? And where exactly?"

Edwin lifted his eyebrows. "Where exactly?"

"Yes. If you could point out where the ache is more prominent? I need to confirm if it's a migraine or if it's a headache like you say. Is the pain all over, or in certain areas?"

"Oh, no. It usually feels like my face is... compressed. It feels like it's behind my eyes, but sometimes, the pain travels to the left side or the right. Sometimes, it's all over."

"And when did this start?"

Edwin inhaled deeply, feeling more comfortable. "Well, I used to live in Minnesota. Back then, I used to think I had these symptoms because I didn't like the environment I lived in. They were mild then, but when we moved to Appleton, it felt as if the symptoms intensified. I like it here, so I don't think it has anything to do with the environment."

"So back then, these symptoms were mild?"

"Yes. I didn't have frequent dizzy spells then. Perhaps I worked too much and that's the cause, but I'm not sure anymore. That's why I'm here."

"Do you sleep well?" Samantha asked, rising to her feet. "How's your sleep schedule?"

Edwin chuckled lightly. "The eye bags, huh? I knew that's what you saw at the door that made you insist that I came in. I do sleep well, actually. I've had no problem sleeping, and I barely wake up during the night. My eyes are always the most tired. That's another reason I'm worried. If sleep isn't the cause of the dark circles, what is?"

"It could be genetics," Samantha said, approaching him. "Dark circles do not always have to do with sleep."

"Oh."

Samantha placed a hand on Edwin's chin and tilted his head upwards. "I'd like to do a quick examination of your eyes, Edwin. Is that, all right?"

Edwin cleared his throat and sat up. "Sure."

"I actually didn't notice the eye bags first at the door," Samantha said, assessing his eyeballs. "Your eyes kept darting left and right. Apart from the headache, have you noticed anything different about your eyes?"

"Well, they itch occasionally and get watery."

"Do you see properly?"

"Define properly," Edwin joked.

"How's your vision?"

"Good," he answered. "I can't see things that are far away, but that's normal, isn't it?"

"Well, it depends on how far away these things are," Samantha said. "What about Rheum in the eye?"

"Rheum?"

"Mucus... that gunk that forms when you sleep for a while," Samantha explained. "Do you get them sometimes?"

"A lot of times, actually. I think I get that more than other people."

Samantha sat back down, but this time something was different. Her expression had changed. Her eyebrows were furrowed, and she sighed deeply. Samantha took her book and wrote while he sat there, uncomfortable with the silence.

Edwin drew in a raggedy breath. His hands had gone cold at the thought that something was wrong. Did Samantha sense a deeper problem? Did she not know what it was? Was she unsure?

"Is there a problem?" Edwin managed to ask.

Samantha set the book down and faced him. "I have to ask you a few questions, Edwin. Unrelated to your symptoms."

"Go for it."

Samantha took another deep breath but forced a smile this time. "Is there any history of blindness in your family?"

Edwin felt as if he had been hit by a train. Blindness!

CHAPTER NINE

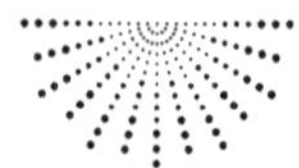

The afternoon was windy. Margaret stood outside the restaurant with her eyes shut. She loved the cool breeze on her face and the whistling sound the wind made. It was even better at night when she gazed at the stars in the sky before going to bed.

It was the day of the dance. Margaret had barely got enough sleep the night before. She was too excited to sleep. As she turned on the bed, Margaret imagined several scenarios in her head. Most of them ended with her spending the evening in Edwin's arms as they slow-danced. She had caught herself blushing several times before she was able to finally fall asleep.

"What are you thinking so deeply about?" Carolyn asked stepping outside.

Margaret gasped and opened her eyes. "You scared me, Carolyn."

"Scared you?" Leticia joined them. "You must have really been thinking about something. Mind if I take a guess?" She chuckled a little and winked.

"Oh, you know I was thinking about Edwin," Margaret said. "You don't have to tease me about it."

"We weren't going to tease you," Carolyn said. "In fact, I'm not in any position to tease anyone right now. I'm really nervous."

They began to slowly walk down the path with their arms interlocked. Margaret was nervous too, but her excitement outweighed it. The picnic she had with Edwin was the best idea she had come up with in a while. Although she was discouraged at the start, things had picked up after she and Edwin really talked. They had talked for over an hour before he began to feel drowsy and they had to leave.

"So, why are you nervous, Carolyn?" Leticia asked. "I see no reason for you to be. You and Sherman see each other every day and you're both clear about your intentions with each other."

"I think so too," Margaret added. "I'm nervous because I'm afraid that what I have with Edwin is temporary. You and Sherman are practically inseparable at this point."

"I'm not nervous because I'm seeing him at the dance," Carolyn explained. "I'm nervous because I think this might be the night Sherman asks me for my hand in marriage."

Margaret and Leticia gasped simultaneously. "What? Are you sure?" Leticia asked.

"I'm not totally sure, but," Carolyn groaned. "I just know. Sherman has been asking me about the dance, about specific things, and all of that. These days, I've noticed that he has gotten more serious with our relationship. We talk about children, marriages, and he always asks me about my view on things. Then he listens like he's trying to take note of the things. I can just tell."

Margaret shrieked. "Oh, I'm so excited. I might just cry if I see Sherman get down on one knee."

"In front of the crowd..." Leticia added.

"With a beautiful ring..." Margaret giggled.

"And a proud smile on his face."

"As he says those words..."

"Will you marry me, Carolyn Darby?"

Margaret and Leticia shrieked again and giggled. It didn't seem like Carolyn was excited, due to the worried look on her face, but Margaret knew she was. Carolyn always doubted everything. She always saw all the pros and the cons of a situation before she made a decision. She was the cautious one. Margaret could understand why Carolyn worried, but she hoped her friend would not let their past stop her from finding happiness.

"Stop looking at me like that," Carolyn said. "Both of you." She put on a mock angry face and shook her head at them before letting her smile show through.

Margaret shrugged her shoulders. "Well, you don't seem thrilled by the idea."

"I am thrilled," Carolyn said. "In fact, when the thought occurred to me that Sherman was going to propose, I was over the moon with happiness. I couldn't sleep. But then, this morning, the usual worrying started and I couldn't help it."

"Won't you say yes to him?" Leticia asked. "Don't tell me you're considering turning Sherman down?"

"Of course not. I'm not crazy." Carolyn shrugged her shoulders as if to say, am I? "I'm just nervous, that's all. I'd love to marry Sherman. I'm just thinking of a solution in case the word of our past misfortunes gets out."

"Oh, do you do anything but worry, Carolyn?" Margaret asked. "That's all you do. Stop and smell the roses, would you?"

Carolyn giggled. "All right. Fine."

Leticia muffled a groan and grabbed her finger. "Ah."

Margaret turned to her. "What is it? Is your finger still hurting?"

Leticia shook her head. "Not much. It just feels like a dull throb, but sometimes I get this sharp pain in it."

"It's been three days, shouldn't you go back to Doctor Randall and let him check if it's healing?" Carolyn asked. "The sharp pain might be a sign of something."

Leticia massaged her neck and chuckled awkwardly. "I'll go. Of course, I'll go."

"Why doesn't it seem like you actually want to go?"

Margaret rolled her eyes. "She's scared of visiting the doctor because she doesn't want to look him in the eyes."

"No, I'm not," Leticia argued. "Why would I be scared of a doctor? I'm not a child."

"You know that's not what she means," Carolyn chipped in. "Put your sentimental feelings aside and go and get your finger examined. You're a nurse, you know the importance of monitoring a wound, don't you?"

"I was a nurse," Leticia said. "But you have a point. I am a nurse, so I can check this myself and make sure it's healing properly. We can't let our skills go to waste now, can we?"

"Leticia," Carolyn called her with a knowing look on her face.

"Fine, I'll go to Doctor Randall's," Leticia said. "But I just can't get over his eyes. I'm not exaggerating, girls. They look just like Dwight's. It completely destabilized me."

"I saw," Margaret said. "You cried like a child."

"I didn't cry like a child. I just sobbed a little, that's all."

"But, if I may ask, Letty," Carolyn said. "Shouldn't that be a good thing? I mean, the fact that something reminds you of Dwight."

"It's not. It should be... I guess, but it's not. That morning, I dreamt of Dwight and it bothered me because it's always the same dream. Then, I saw someone with Dwight's eyes. It's only typical that I freaked out."

"Well, perhaps, your injured finger might be a sign from Dwight. You know, from beyond."

Leticia arched her eyebrows. "What kind of sign?"

"To maybe move on from him," Margaret said. "To stop mourning him. Dwight loved you too. I know he wouldn't want to see you like this."

Leticia shook her head. "I don't know, Maggie."

Margaret paused in her tracks, causing Carolyn and Leticia to stop too.

"Leticia," Margaret started. "Look at Carolyn. Of the three of us, she worries the most. But she was able to open up to someone and fall in love. I met Edwin. And although I have no idea what the future holds, I'm happy now. Don't you want to find your happiness too?"

"Of course, I do." Leticia dropped her head and sighed. "I would like to find happiness too. I thought that this move to Appleton would be a fresh start for me. But then, these dreams of Dwight came back. Perhaps they only stopped because we were going through a lot in Minnesota, and now that we're at peace, it started all over again. I want to be happy, but when I think of how deeply I loved Dwight, I get scared."

Carolyn took a step forward and placed a hand on Leticia's shoulders. "I get it."

Leticia raised her head. "You are worried about people finding out that we worked for Porter Hathaway, right? Well, I'm worried that my love for Dwight and the fact that I nearly shot a man back in Minnesota will scare people away."

"Open your heart, Leticia," Margaret said. "Dwight isn't here anymore, and he'd want you to be happy. Be open to the idea of happiness and see what happens. You're the one still choosing to dwell on the past. Stop it. Both of you. I am so tired of hearing only the depressing things. We deserve to be happy. We keep saying it, but we still worry about these things and it's holding us back."

"Oh, Margaret." Leticia shook her head with a faint smile on her face. "Always the optimist."

"You should be too. We've come a long way to keep talking about the same thing over and over again. Carolyn, I understand your worry, but the more we talk about it, the more it drags us back to square one. Yes, if people found out, it might change their perspective of us, and it might affect Sherman too. Don't you think Sherman knows this? But he still wants to be with you because that's all that matters. Leticia, I know you can't control the dreams you have, but what you can control, is how they affect you. Stop thinking of them as something depressing, and dwell on the good memories. You need to move on. Please. I know I made mistakes in the past, and I am responsible for all the experiences we're currently regretting, but it was the two of you who told me not to let it get me down. How do you think I feel right now when it seems like I'm the only one that's trying to be happy?"

"Well, you're not responsible for the dreams I'm having so that shouldn't burden you. I might be going crazy, but I can't be too sure yet," Leticia joked.

Margaret let out a frustrated sigh and tilted her head sideways. "Letty. Come on. I'm being serious here."

"We know," Carolyn chimed in. "I promise, I am not letting these things hold me back. Sure, I worry about them, but I love Sherman, and I want to be with him."

"And it might not seem like it, but I'm trying to move on. Trust me," Leticia said. "We'll work everything out together. Like we always do."

Margaret nodded. "I'd like that."

Margaret locked their arms together and they continued. The sun was setting, creating a magnificent display that took her breath away. One other thing Margaret loved was to drink in the orange sky at this time of day. She also hid the fact that she still carried the burden of guilt for putting them in this situation in the first place.

There was so much on her mind, but Margaret held out the hope that the pain of the war and their ordeal in Minnesota would be a distant memory at the end of the night. She hoped that the dance was memorable enough to bury the distress they were all feeling.

"Maggie, you're a terrible dancer," Leticia stated, somewhat out of the blue.

"So?" Margaret retorted.

"Aren't you worried that you're going to embarrass yourself?"

"No." Margaret smiled. "Well, maybe a little. But I'll be in Edwin's arms and my mind will not be on embarrassment."

Leticia chuckled. "Oh, the power of love."

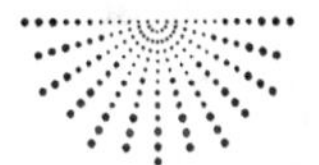

CHAPTER TEN

"Carolyn!"

Sherman's voice stopped the ladies in their tracks as they walked into the yard. The church had gladly volunteered the building for the town dance to hold. It was another reason for the members of the community to admire Sherman and his parishioners. Margaret felt proud to be part of a selfless cause. The church was her second home.

"Oh, someone's beau seems to have been waiting for her," Leticia teased.

"Stop, he'll hear you." Carolyn blushed.

Leticia waved her hand in the air. "So? Sherman adores you. The way he looks at you alone makes me want to bite my fingers and shriek in excitement. It's nice to see. I'm really happy for you, Carolyn. You found your soulmate."

"Stop, Letty. You're going to make me blush. What would Sherman think if he sees my cheeks flush crimson like a young girl?"

"Carolyn, you're already blushing," Leticia noted with a chuckle.

"Oh, my." She giggled. "You both can head in without me. I'll catch up."

Margaret and Leticia stifled their giggles as Carolyn hurried over to Sherman's side. They kept walking towards the entrance, keeping their eyes on Carolyn. They loved to tease each other about the littlest of things. Given that there wasn't a lot to make them laugh, Margaret and her friends found their amusement in each other. It had always been like that between them since they met.

The dance began almost as soon as they walked in. The pews had been moved out or stacked at the side to accommodate everyone and to match the tone of the evening. Margaret hadn't noticed how spacious the room was until she saw the cleared floor.

Excitement coursed through her as she scanned the room and her gaze fell on a trio of fiddlers in the corner. She smiled, as they touched their bows to the strings and began to play a jaunty tune.

"I have a good feeling about the evening, Letty," Margaret said. "This tune just makes me want to shut my eyes and prance around the dance floor."

"Well, don't," Leticia told her. "Especially not with your eyes closed. You're most definitely going to fall on your face."

Margaret blew raspberries at Leticia. "I'll do it anyway. But with Edwin, so he catches me when I trip."

Leticia shook her head. "Speaking of Edwin..."

Margaret followed Leticia's gaze and she locked eyes with Edwin in the corner of the room. Edwin waved at her, smiling sheepishly and she waved back.

"Letty, see you later," Margaret said excitedly.

"See you later. Try not to have too much fun."

Margaret scurried over to Edwin's side without sparing a minute to reply to Leticia's remark. He looked handsome in his sky-blue shirt, black jeans, and suspenders. He also had on polished black shoes and a hat. But most importantly, his smile was the best look on him.

"Good evening, Edwin," Margaret said. "How are you?"

Edwin took off his hat and bowed, taking her hand and planting a kiss on it. "I'm very well, Maggie. How are you this evening?"

"I'm fine too. Thank you for asking. Are you feeling better now?"

Edwin's smile dwindled, it was as if he was forcing it to remain on his face and nerves fluttered in her stomach like angry bees.

"I am. I got some rest, and my workload has reduced, so I'm much better now."

"Oh, that's good to hear." Margaret smiled, relieved, and yet, there was a note of worry in his eyes. She pushed her doubts to the side. She was worried herself and seeing things that weren't there.

"Where's Carolyn?" Edwin asked, scanning the room. "I only see Leticia. I'd like to apologize to her again for last time."

"She's outside speaking to Sherman," she answered. "And I told you not to think too much of it. Carolyn has forgotten about it."

"Oh, but I haven't," Edwin said. "I think about it from time to time. I would like to apologize to her before I…" Edwin paused and smiled. "I'd like to apologize."

"Well, if you insist. You can catch up with her after the dance," Margaret said. "Is that all right?"

Edwin nodded. "It is. Thank you, Maggie. You look beautiful tonight."

Margaret glanced at her peach gown and blushed. "Thank you, Edwin. You look handsome yourself."

"Thank you, Maggie," he replied and took her hand. "You know, I often think about the picnic we had. That afternoon at the small meadow. It was the most fun I have had in a while."

"Me too. I think about it all the time and I loved every moment. We can always go back there whenever and continue where we left off."

Edwin kept his head bowed as he fiddled with Margaret's hand. He looked like he was thinking about something. Margaret clenched her other hand into a fist.

She didn't want to go back to worrying about him again. They had just rekindled their relationship.

"Edwin, are you all right?" she forced herself to ask for a kernel of fear was growing inside of her. Something was wrong!

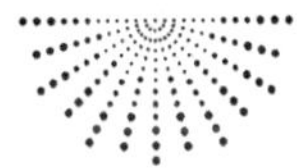

Edwin lifted his head with a smile on his face. He brought his fingers to Margaret's hair and stroked it. "You know, you have beautiful hair, Margaret. This bright, red color. During the picnic, I couldn't stop staring at it. I loved how radiantly it shone in the sunlight."

"Thank you, Edwin," Margaret said softly.

His words had melted her completely. So much so that she got weak in the knees. It wasn't every day she got complimented for her looks. But somehow, she always received compliments whenever she was with Edwin. He knew the right things to say to put her in the best mood. And with every sweet word that came from his lips, coupled with the sincerity in his eyes, Margaret liked Edwin more and more.

"I want to keep that memory close to my heart forever. I never want to forget it."

Margaret squinted her eyes. "A memory? Edwin, you don't have to keep that one memory when we can make lots more."

Edwin only smiled and continued to stroke Margaret's hair. Confused was an understatement for how she was feeling at that moment. Edwin was there, but then again... he wasn't.

Margaret gently placed her hand on Edwin's, stopping him from stroking her hair. "Edwin," she said softly. "We'll see each other every day, and you will see me countless times in the sun. Why does one nice day need to be kept as a memory? We can have many more moments. Our entire future is on the horizon. It's going to be beautiful, filled with many colors, and worth it all. You'll see."

Edwin pulled his hand away and a frown formed on his face. He took a step back and lowered his head to hide his face. The sudden change in demeanor scared

Margaret. Perhaps she had said something wrong. She was too forward, she was going too quickly.

"Did I overstep in some way?" Margaret asked. "I'm so sorry if I did. I was just trying to make a point."

Edwin ran his hand through his own hair, roughly. "I wasn't trying to make you uncomfortable by stepping back. I just felt diz-"

Edwin paused and clenched his jaw. He reached for Margaret's hand and shook his head. "No. You didn't overstep. Come on, let's dance. I promised you that this night was going to be memorable, and I plan on keeping that promise. Shall we dance?"

Margaret nodded and allowed Edwin to lead her to the dance floor. She just couldn't shake the feeling that something was wrong. That he wasn't being his usual self because he was keeping something from her. He had developed a habit of starting a sentence, pausing after a few words, and ending it with 'never mind.' Still, Margaret didn't want to make a mountain out of a molehill.

"Please don't laugh," Edwin said as he took her into his arms. "I did warn you that I'm a terrible dancer. This might be awkward."

Margaret giggled. "I can't promise much either. I figured I'd just follow your lead but if you aren't confident then we might make a fool of ourselves but who cares?"

Edwin chuckled too. "I've been practicing. Or at least, I tried to practice. I didn't have much success. However, I did get the hang of it after the seventh try."

Edwin pulled Margaret close, and at the same time, she moved forward rapidly too, causing them to bump each other. They laughed it off and tried to adjust their stance again. Edwin was cautious with his hand around her back. His breathing was raggedy, and he took in deep breaths every few seconds.

"And I thought I was the nervous one," Margaret joked.

"Is it obvious?" Edwin asked.

"Very." She giggled. "But that makes two of us. I think it's pretty sweet that you practiced your dancing for me. If I had more time off work at the restaurant I would have practiced too."

"You're doing great," Edwin said, watching Margaret's feet as they moved to the tune. "See, we're doing it."

"I'm copying you. That's all I'm doing."

Margaret cherished how she fit so perfectly in his arms. Edwin looked at her and handled her with so much care. She didn't worry about how ungraceful their dancing looked to other people, Margaret was just happy to be in his arms.

"Yes, but it looks good, doesn't it?" Edwin asked.

Margaret nodded. "It does. I would be more than happy to match your rhythm for the rest of my days."

The same look again. Edwin looked pleased with her words at first, but then his eyebrows furrowed, and he couldn't even force a smile. Something was wrong, but she was confused as to what it was. Heat rose up the back of her head when Edwin lowered his head and emitted a heavy sigh. His expressions were driving her to the brink of insanity.

"Edwin, what is it?" Margaret summoned the courage to ask. "I know I'm not reading meaning into nothing. Tell me. Is something wrong, or are you just tired, still?"

"I'm fine, Maggie," Edwin said blankly.

Margaret sighed. "Why am I tired of hearing you say that?"

Edwin lifted his hand and with his fingers, he stroked Margaret's hair. "Well, you shouldn't be. I don't want you to worry about me. Remember when I told you that I didn't like it?"

Margaret nodded. "You said it makes you feel like a burden. But you'll never be a burden to me, Edwin. I care about you, that's why I worry. That's how it's supposed to work."

The change in his facial expression led Margaret to believe that she might have overstepped again. Seeing Edwin with a mix of sadness and seriousness plastered all over his face made her tense. She missed the old Edwin. The one she talked to every single day during the time they journeyed to Appleton.

But something had changed. Her relationship with Carolyn and Leticia had made it so that Margaret believed it was normal to be aware of every single change in their lives. She knew everything about them, and they talked about everything together. Perhaps, that was the reason Margaret found it strange that Edwin was keeping things to himself when she was there for him to share his thoughts.

Margaret lifted her head after a while and met the same expression on Edwin's face. She took a step back, unable to think of what to say or do. Usually, Margaret was comfortable with the silence between her and Edwin. But she felt a need to say something in this moment. To be sure that she had not overstepped.

Just then, Edwin pulled her back into the dance, causing Margaret to gasp. He leaned in, casually placing his head on her shoulder as he swayed with her in his arms. It was better like this. Dancing without looking Edwin in the eye. At least she could sway in the arms of the man she cared about without feeling the urge to assess every emotion that ran across his face.

Margaret traced Edwin's back with her fingers and shut her eyes. It was her turn to worry. She feared that she was losing him even though she was wrapped in his arms.

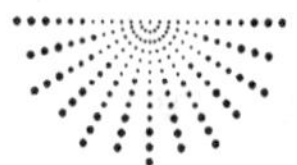

CHAPTER TWELVE

"Why aren't we dancing inside with the others, Sherman?"

Her gut feeling was right. Carolyn had not confirmed it yet, but she was sure. Sherman was an open book in the literal sense of the word. First, he made a big deal about her attending the dance, then when she arrived, he pulled her aside for a walk around the church.

Also, Sherman was smiling, a lot more than usual. He was in a very good mood. If he had received any news in the past few days that could get him in that mood, Carolyn knew he would have shared it with her since they told each other everything. But he had not. Which meant, Sherman was anticipating something. The thought of what it was sent tingles running down her spine.

"Oh, I just thought a walk would be nice," Sherman answered. "How are you?"

Carolyn placed both hands behind her back, trying to maintain her composure. "I'm fine, thank you. How was your day?"

"Well, I spent it helping the others prepare for the dance. There was, surprisingly, a lot to do. But we were able to pull it off in time. Thankfully."

"You did a good job, with everything," Carolyn said. "You should be proud."

Sherman smiled. "Why, thank you, Carolyn. That means so much."

Sometimes, Carolyn felt the urge to brag about Sherman. She would joke to Leticia and Margaret about how she might have been a hero in her past life to deserve someone like Sherman in her current one. He appeared from nowhere, a knight in shining armor, and had saved her on numerous occasions. Everything was pointing to the fact that they were meant to be together. It couldn't have been a coincidence. They were meant to meet each other that night.

"Tell me something, Carolyn," Sherman started. "Do you like it here in Appleton?"

Carolyn tilted her head to the side. "Do I like the community?"

"Are you happy? Do you really like your job, or are you just putting up with it? Do you like the people? Are you happy here?"

Carolyn stared at the ground with a wide smile on her face. "I would be happy anywhere as long as I have three things."

"What things?"

"Well, not things, but... Margaret, Leticia, and you." Carolyn bit her lower lip. "Since I have those three things, you could say that I'm happy."

Sherman paused for a second, then cleared his throat. "My love, that doesn't answer the question."

"I really think it does," she argued.

"No, it doesn't. I want to know what you think about the community and your job. Not how comfortable you are because of the people you're so used to being around."

"Well, I think that I'm happy because I have…"

"Carolyn," Sherman stopped her, chuckling. "Would you just answer the question?"

Carolyn's smile widened. "Fine then. Compared to Minnesota? This place is heaven. People here are so nice to me, and I truly like my job, Sherman. I learned a lot of new recipes too, and Penny loves to tell us stories about her grandmother and how she started the restaurant. I'm happy here. But I do worry. I know it's a bad habit, but I've always been like this."

Sherman's forehead furrowed. "What do you worry about?"

They both reached the fence and stopped. Carolyn leaned on the wood, staring into the darkness. "Minnesota," Carolyn stated. "You know I will never stop thanking you for saving us?"

"You know, I've literarily begged you to stop?"

Carolyn shook her head. "I'm not going to. It's a big deal, Sherman. However, even though we are miles away from that place, I still get a bad feeling when I think of all we endured. A part of me fears that Porter and Brandon will make good on their promise and come back to stir up more trouble for us. You heard what Porter said that night in the forest. He said it wasn't over.

Sherman placed both hands on Carolyn's shoulders and turned her to him. "Carolyn, those are just the words of a man with a bruised ego. He lost, hence he felt the need to have the last word."

"Well, the other part of me knows that, and I hate myself for worrying, but I always do."

"Relax. I think that vile man's words were all empty threats and bluster. You feel like this because these men are always up to something devious. But I think, that right now, they are likely inventing other schemes many miles away. Ones that don't concern us."

Carolyn exhaled slowly. "You really think so?"

"I do." Sherman nodded. "I really do, we were too much trouble. Cowards like that prefer easier pickings. I know that telling you this will probably do nothing, but stop worrying. We are here, together, and all I want is to marry you, Carolyn Darby. Soon. I need you to be my wife."

Her heart leaped in her chest, had he just said that?

Carolyn watched Sherman pull out a ring from the pocket of his trousers. Her heart skipped a beat and then raced like a wild horse that had escaped from its captors. It soared like an eagle in the sky. It was really happening.

"You knew I was going to do this today, didn't you?" Sherman asked.

Carolyn giggled, sniffing back the tears. "I did. How'd you know?"

"You've had this suspicious look in your eyes since yesterday. I could tell you knew I was up to something. You're an open book, Carolyn," Sherman said.

"Looks who's talking." Carolyn laughed, her gaze never leaving the ring.

"So?" Sherman said softly. "Will you marry me, Carolyn?"

Carolyn bit her lower lip to restrain herself from rushing her answer. Margaret's words kept repeating in her head. It was all right to want something for yourself. It was all right to want to be happy.

But at what cost?

"Sherman, you have been doing so much good for the town," Carolyn said. "Everyone loves you. You're a saint.

You're exemplary. People look up to you. If people knew the sordid details of my past, I am sure they won't look at me in the same light that they see me now. Am I truly cut out to be your wife, when I risk jeopardizing your reputation?"

CHAPTER THIRTEEN

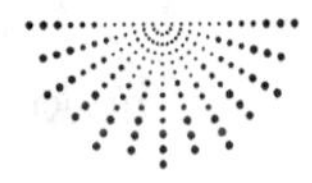

"You did nothing wrong, Carolyn," Sherman replied.

"I know that. But it doesn't mean people would believe it."

"I will never let what happened in Minnesota be held against you," Sherman said sternly. "I love you, Carolyn, and I need you. I would be proud to call you my wife. If you need me to confess my love to you by standing on the top of a mountain and yelling so the whole world can hear, then I'll do it."

Carolyn giggled as tears welled up in her eyes. "Oh, I keep asking myself every day what I did to deserve you, Sherman."

"Marry me, Carolyn."

Carolyn stared at the ring and took in a deep breath. Perhaps it was time to throw caution to the wind and go for what she wanted. Who was she kidding? Her lips and her heart were on totally different pages. Carolyn wanted to marry this man. She knew it from the first day she saw him.

As she opened her mouth to speak, Carolyn heard the church door open. She glanced at it, hoping to take only a quick look, but Margaret appeared. Carolyn watched Margaret walk down the stairwell with deflated steps. Her eyes weren't focused and she looked like she'd seen a ghost.

"Is that Margaret?" Sherman questioned. "I think she's going to fall, Carolyn."

"I think so too. Would you excuse me, Sherman?"

"I'll come with you."

Carolyn hurried over to Margaret's side. She had never seen Margaret that lifeless before.

"Maggie?" Carolyn called out to her. "Margaret, is everything all right? What's wrong?"

Margaret stared into space with furrowed eyebrows and squinted eyes. "I... I..."

"Where's Edwin? Where's Leticia? What happened, Maggie? Why do you look like this?"

Margaret finally turned to Carolyn. "I don't know, Carolyn. I'm not sure. I was dancing with Edwin one second, and the next... he left me."

"What do you mean?" Carolyn asked. "He left?"

"I felt him drop his hand and pull away from me, so I lifted my eyes to look at him, but he was looking at something else. I followed his gaze and discovered that he was staring at someone else. This lady. I've seen her before. She's always with Doctor Randall. Edwin locked eyes with her and walked away from me."

Carolyn scoffed in disbelief. "He walked away?"

Margaret nodded.

"Well, perhaps he knows her or something," Carolyn stuttered. "It might not mean anything, Maggie."

"Yes, it does, Carolyn." Margaret's voice quivered. "Edwin has been acting very strange in the past month. He speaks of me like I'm a distant memory, and his smile wanes when I talk about a future with him. It means something."

"Margaret, try to relax," Sherman told her. "The lady in question is Samantha Randall, Doctor Randall's daughter. She's a doctor too."

"What would Edwin want with Samantha?" Margaret asked. "You're his closest friend and he tells you everything. You should know what is going on with him because there is something and I know it. I can feel it but he won't tell me."

Sherman massaged his forehead. "Honestly, I've also been thinking the same thing for the past couple of days. Edwin claims he's only tired and he just needs rest."

"It's more than that," Margaret argued. "You know it's more than that. I reckon he is hiding something from me. And it has something to do with that lady." Tears formed in her eyes and she shook her head willing them not to fall.

"It might not be what you think, Maggie," Carolyn said.

"Have you seen the lady in question, Carolyn?" Margaret asked. "She's prettier than me. She's slim, and Sherman says she's a doctor. Carolyn, I'm not an idiot. I might be incredibly naïve, but I'm not an idiot."

They were standing in the doorway, where everyone could hear them. Carolyn quickly scanned the area, figuring that it was best to stand outside and talk.

"We're blocking the door, Maggie," Carolyn said. "Let's talk over at the fence."

Margaret nodded and let Carolyn and Sherman lead her down the steps. Carolyn didn't want to jump to any conclusions, mainly because Edwin was a good person and he vowed not to hurt Margaret. There had to be an explanation.

Just as they passed by the corner, Carolyn heard people speaking in hushed tones. When they all paused, she knew Margaret and Sherman heard it too. It was coming from the side of the church, and when Carolyn squinted her eyes to focus, she discovered that it was two people, standing close to each other.

"Is that... Edwin?" Margaret said.

It was Edwin. Carolyn recognized his hat immediately after Margaret said it. Just as she was about to suggest that they go their own way and talk, Samantha took Edwin in her arms. She hugged him and he hugged her back.

"Maggie..."

Carolyn could barely get a word in before Margaret charged toward them. She was always the impulsive one. Not stopping to think her decisions through before she made them.

"What is going on here?" Margaret demanded, standing with her fists clenched at her sides.

CHAPTER FOURTEEN

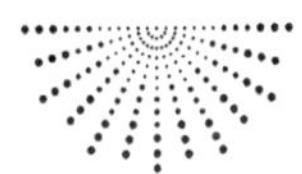

The feeling of his palpitating heart made Edwin dizzy. He lifted his head to the night sky, shut his eyes, and took in a deep breath to calm himself.

It wasn't supposed to happen like this. But then again, he had no clue how he was going to break the news to Margaret. He had pondered on it every day since he had the discussion with Samantha about his eyesight. He had gone through different scenarios, but none played out how he wanted them to. Perhaps, this was karma for keeping the truth to himself instead of confiding in Margaret.

"Edwin!" Margaret called out to him sternly. "Would you please say something?"

Margaret was furious. That much was obvious. She always looked sad when she was angry about something.

"Edwin!" Margaret called out to him again.

"Edwin, say something," Carolyn chipped in, taking a step forward.

"Hello. My name is Samantha Randall. My father is the local doctor here in town," Samantha said in Edwin's stead.

"Edwin," Margaret called him for the third time.

Things were happening faster than Edwin hoped they would. He thought he had more time to spend with Margaret and create more memories with her that he could cherish. But it wasn't a big cause for concern. He had enough memories of her from the moment they met three months ago.

"This is a big misunderstanding," Samantha said. "Edwin and I are friends. He came to the clinic a few days ago for an examination. That is how we met."

Margaret finally turned to Samantha. "I want to believe you, Miss, but I cannot take your word for it. I need to hear the truth from Edwin's own lips. Let him tell me why he left me on the dance floor to come here to embrace you."

"I apologize for that," Samantha continued. "But I was only consoling him, nothing else. I'm sorry if you misunderstood."

Edwin wondered if all of this was going to affect his duties in the church. If Sherman saw him in a different light. Was he really all right to become the bad person?

"Let me ask you this, Miss," Margaret said to Samantha.

"Please, call me Sam," Samantha insisted. "Or Sammy. We're the same age, and I don't think we should speak so formally."

Margaret crossed her arms. "I'd rather not. I want to know what you were consoling Edwin about."

Samantha glanced at Edwin and their eyes met. She looked away and fiddled with her fingers. Edwin was sure she wasn't going to tell. He had made her promise not to mention it to anyone. At least until they couldn't hide it anymore.

"It's not my place to tell, I'm sorry," Samantha said.

"But it's your place to console him?" Margaret retorted.

"Maggie," Carolyn cautioned her. "Calm yourself."

Margaret threw her hands in the air. "Edwin? Why aren't you saying anything? Or do I not deserve a reply from you?"

Edwin summoned all the courage he could garner to look Margaret in the eye. "Sam and I, we – she's a doctor. When I realized that my constant fatigue and heavy eyes weren't quite normal, I sought out Dr. Randall at the clinic. He wasn't there but Miss Randall told me that she was a doctor also and she examined me, and was there to talk to me... let's just say I feel a bit better after meeting her."

Margaret scoffed. "She was there to talk to you? What am I? A sack of rice? Edwin, I asked you constantly, I literarily begged you to talk to me. But you said not to worry, that you were fine. But what are you saying now? This lady was there to talk to you?"

Samantha took a step forward and placed a hand on Edwin's arm. "Edwin, you're not making the situation any better," she whispered to him.

"Let me handle this. Please," Edwin whispered back. "Just go along with whatever I say. That way it's better for everyone."

"Everyone but yourself," Samantha said. "Edwin, don't push people away. You'll need them."

"Why are you both whispering again?" Margaret asked impatiently. "Edwin, is Samantha just a friend or not? Don't beat around the bush and just tell me the truth."

"Yes," Edwin stated. "She is a friend, Margaret. But now, I think I want to explore a relationship with Sam. She understands me."

The look of sheer shock was evident on Margaret's face. Even as the words fell from his lips, Edwin felt his blood chill. Margaret turned to stare at Carolyn as if she was seeking assistance.

"I'm sorry, Margaret," Edwin added. "I'm sorry it had to end like this."

Margaret glared at him and took slow steps in his direction. "Why did you say all of those things to me then? Just a few minutes ago, you" – Margaret drew in a raggedy breath and shut her eyes. – "Am I dreaming? Is this a joke, Edwin? Because it makes no sense at all."

"It makes sense to me," Edwin said. "We had something, Margaret, but we lost it. As harsh as it might sound, it's the truth. We can't be together. It's unfair to you."

Then it was over; Margaret felt as if her legs would buckle, as if tears would stream down her face and she would wail like a bereaved child... but she wouldn't. No, he would not see how much he had shattered her heart. He would not have that satisfaction.

Raising her head, she pushed back her shoulders and nodded. "So be it."

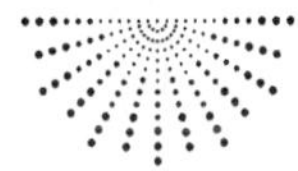

CHAPTER FIFTEEN

"Edwin, you cannot be serious," Sherman said. "Just three days ago, you were learning how to dance so you'd give Margaret a memorable night. Is this your idea of memorable?"

It wasn't supposed to happen this way. Edwin had truly intended to make the night memorable for Margaret, and especially for himself. But fate had other plans.

"Edwin," Margaret called him softly, reaching for his hand. "What is the matter? This is unlike you. I don't understand why you're acting like this."

Edwin pulled his hand away before Margaret could touch it. "I would like to explore the possibility of a relationship with Sam. I should have told you earlier, but I couldn't. Let's not make this harder than it needs to be."

Margaret went silent, but Edwin could hear her labored breathing. It started off slow, and then it increased to the point that he could tell she was fuming with rage. Edwin instinctively lifted his head to look at her, but a sound slap across the face sent him staggering backward. He groaned and stared at Margaret in disbelief. Not once in his numerous scenarios, did he imagine that Margaret would slap him.

"Do not seek me out ever again, Edwin Grant," she sobbed. "You are a liar and a deceiver, and I never want to see you again."

With that Margaret stormed away from the church, wiping her tears as she walked. Edwin's first instinct was to follow her, but he clenched his fingers into a fist to restrain himself. The more he tried to convince himself that it was for the best, the more it hurt.

Carolyn walked up to him with her arms crossed. She glared at him and shook her head in disappointment.

Edwin exhaled forcefully through his mouth. "Carolyn, about the other day. I'd like to apologize..."

"Oh, save your apology, Edwin," Carolyn rasped. "Now, I don't know what in the world is going on with you, and why you thought hurting Margaret was a good idea, but leave my friend alone. You know, she knew something was wrong somewhere but she chose to come to you, to be with you and fight for what you both had. But you took it upon yourself to hurt her. I won't let you get a second chance at it, so please, stay away from us."

Edwin lowered his head as Carolyn ran after Margaret. Sherman was still standing in front of him, and Edwin was terrified to see the expression on his face. He had never seen Sherman angry before.

"I am utterly disappointed, Edwin," Sherman said calmly.

It wasn't anger. It was a lot worse. Sherman was sad. Disappointed. The things Edwin did to push Margaret away had affected everything and everyone. And he feared that there was no way to remedy the situation. How was he going to live in Appleton after this?

"No one is faulting you for wanting to be with someone else," Sherman continued. "We are all human, and we have choices and decisions to make. However, this was cold. Where is your compassion? Is this the best route you could have taken to get what you want? You know that this doesn't just affect you as a person. It affects everyone around you. It's sad, Edwin. Whatever you could talk to Samantha about, and find solace, you could have talked to me about it too. We've known each other for years Edwin and I have never seen this side of you."

Edwin bit his tongue, hoping that the pain would prevent the tears that were threatening to fall. Sherman had stopped talking, and all that was left were the slaps of his feet on the ground. He was all alone now. He had let all his friends down.

"This is my fault," Samantha said. "I shouldn't have hugged you. I am so sorry things ended this way, Edwin."

"It's all right," Edwin responded.

"But you shouldn't…"

"Sam, I don't want to talk about it, please. It would feel like reliving it and I really don't want to do that. I really wish things turned out differently. It shouldn't have happened like this. I still had many memories I wanted to create with Margaret before the imminent darkness came. I wanted us to dance throughout the night, and be the last ones to leave the floor. I wanted to walk her back home and hug her goodnight. This night was supposed to be memorable."

"It could have been. If only you told them we were just friends," Samantha retorted. "You really didn't have to hurt Margaret like that."

"It is the right end for everyone involved," Edwin said. "I'd hate to burden them. Not after what they have done for me. It would be... unfair."

"And what you just did is fair?"

"Sam, don't."

Samantha put both hands in the air. "Sorry. Once again, I apologize for how the night ended, and for how miserable you are going to be henceforth. Because you've pushed your friends away at this crucial point in your life. But I'll try and understand from your perspective. Do you need me to walk you home?"

Edwin shook his head. "I need to be alone right now."

Leticia appeared out of nowhere, panting. She stared at both of them and scanned the yard. "Oh, hi, Edwin. How are you? And where is everyone? I can't find Carolyn or Margaret or Sherman. Last I checked, Maggie was with you."

Edwin scratched the back of his head. "They left."

Leticia raised her eyebrows. "They left?"

"Yes. They left," he stated.

"That is weird," Leticia said, confused. "Maggie really wanted to have the last dance with you. She wouldn't leave in the middle of the dance. And they didn't tell me? Why?"

"I think it's better if you talk to the both of them," Edwin said.

"You see, this is all because they both have partners. They think it's all right to leave me all by myself with my injured finger. I didn't even want to come to the dance in the first place." Leticia groaned. "See you later, Edwin. Take care of yourself. You don't look too well."

Samantha clicked her tongue as she watched Leticia run out of the church. "If only she knew what you just did to her friend."

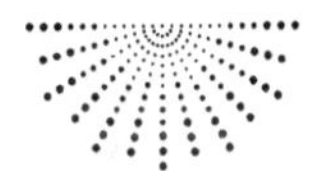

CHAPTER SIXTEEN

"I'm so sorry, Maggie. I didn't know," Leticia cooed. "I would have smacked Edwin across the face if I knew he broke your heart this cruelly."

The night before was the slowest one Leticia had experienced in a long time. They had not gotten a wink of sleep and it was already morning. Margaret had cried all night, nonstop. At one point, Leticia was concerned for her friend's wellbeing. Margaret sobbed so much that she lost her voice.

Leticia hated to see Margaret that way. She had experienced something similar when she lost Dwight but seeing someone else go through it scared her. Was that how she looked when she cried all night and refused to get up in the morning? Was that how broken she was? How hopeless? She couldn't quite remember.

"Where's Carolyn?" Margaret asked with a cracked voice.

Leticia held Margaret in her arms. She and Carolyn had taken turns to comfort Margaret during the night. No matter how much they tried, Margaret didn't stop wailing.

"She went to get you water to drink, honey," Leticia cooed.

"You don't have to speak to me like I'm a baby, Letty," Margaret said. "I'm heartbroken, not fatally wounded."

Leticia scoffed. "Sounds like the same thing to me."

Margaret groaned and sat up. "Why? That's all I could think of throughout the night. Why? Is it because she's prettier than me?"

"Maggie, no one is prettier than you."

Margaret scoffed. "You're just saying that."

"Show me another red-head in this town with pretty blue eyes and a killer smile, then we can talk," Leticia argued. "Don't let anyone tell you anything. I might not have noticed the face of the girl in question because I was focused on Edwin, but let me tell you this. You are prettier, with curves in the right places and you have the best heart, Maggie. Don't let this steal your confidence."

Margaret wiped away the tears as quickly as they rolled down her cheeks. "It's just, Edwin is the second man to do this to me, and it hurts more than the last one because I really loved him. He left me for a lady he met days ago. Can you believe that?"

"Who is this lady anyway?" Leticia asked.

"Her name is Sam," Margaret said. "She works with Doctor Randall."

"Why have I never heard of her?" Leticia mumbled. "Where did she come from?"

"Who?"

Carolyn walked into the room carrying a plate of porridge and a glass of water. She set it down on the table by the bed and sat next to Margaret.

"Sam," Margaret answered. "Letty doesn't know who she is."

"It doesn't matter," Carolyn said, waving a hand in the air.

"Yes, it does," Leticia argued. "We need to know more about her. What did Edwin see in her that made him ruin the beautiful thing he had going with Maggie."

"It doesn't matter," Carolyn insisted. "I told Edwin that I don't want him seeking Maggie out anymore. The harm he has done is enough. If I had known, I would have stopped you from going on that picnic with him. I should have taken his rude tone that day at the church as a sign."

"I just knew something was wrong. I sensed it," Margaret sobbed. "There were clear signs. He didn't think to visit me for a whole month. He never made mention of our future together... there were signs. But I chose to dwell on his promises to change and be better. I thought I could fix things. I thought I could fix him. I wanted to be his happy place, you know? But he had the audacity to tell me he found someone else that understood him. That's all I ever tried to do... but he never let me in."

"Stop, Maggie. Stop thinking about it. You're only going to hurt yourself more," Carolyn said.

"She's right. It might not seem like it, but it's good that you learned the truth sooner rather than later," Leticia chipped in.

"I always try to be optimistic. Perhaps, that's my problem. Maybe I should be rational like you Carolyn, or be constantly doubtful like you, Letty."

"Ouch," Leticia said. "I can be rational and optimistic too."

"Maggie, don't think for a second, that we will allow this heartbreak to change you. Do you know how many times I wished that I was as hopeful and optimistic about everything as you are? You don't allow worrying to stop you from getting what you want. That's bravery. You are not losing your spark. We won't allow it."

Margaret rested her head on the wall. "I think I want to go home, girls. New Hampshire wasn't the best place to live, but at least it was the least problematic. We could all live together in my aunt's house. Let's head back east. I can't do this anymore. Happiness might as well come knocking on my door. I'm done trying to look for it."

"We're not going back to New Hampshire because of this, Maggie," Carolyn told her. "Appleton is our home now. We have to figure out a way to make it work."

"But you're the one that's worried our secret will come out and people would hate us. If we moved back to New Hampshire, we won't have to worry about that."

"But we would have to worry about Porter Hathaway. He knows that address," Carolyn said.

Maggie felt a cold chill run down her spine. There was that!

CHAPTER SEVENTEEN

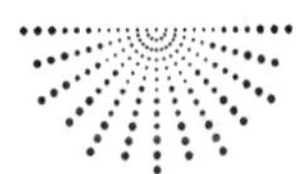

Margaret pushed the feeling of dread away. She had to leave here, she had to get away from Edwin; seeing him with Sam would be too painful. "Ooh, Porter is behind us, Carolyn. And even if you both don't want to move back home with me, I'll just go alone. What I know is that I want to be far away from this part of the world. Far away from Edwin so I can forget him."

Leticia was ready to hop on that idea, but not just yet. They were comfortable here in Appleton, but the circumstances changed after Margaret's heartbreak. If one of them was unhappy, then the three of them were unhappy. However, Leticia wasn't planning on going anywhere until she got all the facts of the still befuddling story straight.

They were talking about Edwin. The Edwin, who was practically obsessed with the shadow of Margaret. Something had changed, and Leticia had a feeling that the Sam in question had something to do with it… but something told her that it was not as the other woman.

Leticia sprang to her feet. "Maggie, eat your porridge. I need to go somewhere. I'll be back."

"Where are you going?" Carolyn asked.

"I'll tell you when I get back," she answered. "Make sure Maggie eats her porridge."

Her first stop was the doctor's house. Margaret said Sam worked there, so Leticia hoped she would meet her. She had an excuse too, so it was convenient. Her injury hadn't been examined in days. Leticia planned to open with it, and then dive deeper into the conversation and find out the kind of lady this Sam was.

Once she reached the doctor's, Leticia found that the door was left open. Without a second thought, she strolled into the clinic, walking with light steps.

The sight she beheld caused her to gasp. Leticia brought her hand to her mouth and covered it. Oliver was embracing a lady, Leticia guessed it was Sam, tightly. He stroked her hair, down her back and they rocked back and forth. Red with rage, Leticia stormed toward them.

"How foolish can you be!" she yelled.

Oliver broke the hug in time to receive a resounding slap across the face from Leticia. He placed a hand on his cheek and stared at her with wide eyes. Sam gasped and rushed to his side.

"What is the meaning of this?" Samantha demanded.

"What gives you the right to hit me, Leticia?" Oliver questioned, still pretty shaken.

"How can you be in love with a woman who is already sniffing around someone else?" Leticia rasped. "Did you not know, or did you choose to play blind? Just yesterday, she was the reason my friend had her heart broken. Now, look what we have here. Sam, or whatever your name is, with another man. How foolish can you be, Doctor Randall? And how callous can you be, Sam?"

"Listen, I don't know what you think you know, but Samantha here is my daughter," Oliver said. "Regardless of that, you have no right to walk into my clinic and slap me across the face just because you are angry about something that has absolutely nothing to do with me. Do you understand?"

It was then that Leticia took a step back to really look at their faces. And now that she was seeing and thinking clearly, she quickly found the resemblance. Margaret had failed to mention that Sam was Oliver Randall's daughter. But Leticia couldn't blame her. Her friend was going through a lot.

But that explanation was not going to suffice for an apology. How was she going to explain to Oliver that she was sentimental because he reminded her so much of the love of her life? That when she saw him stroking another woman's hair – coupled with the fact that Leticia had spent the night tending to a broken heart – the sight made her jealous. She had no idea what came over her, and she had acted on pure impulse. Her brain had just stopped processing information.

"I admit I overstepped, but I..."

"Please leave," Oliver asked.

Leticia tilted her head. "I didn't just barge in here. I came here for a purpose. And I admit that I overstepped my..."

"Leticia, I would appreciate it if you left," Oliver said. "You interfered, rudely, with something that didn't concern you, and you raised your hand to me without cause. It's safe to say I know the type of person you are, and I will not have such people in my clinic."

"The type of person?" Leticia scoffed. "I admit that I made a mistake because I thought you were taking advantage... or rather being taken advantage of. That's why I stepped in. Would you let me apologize?"

"I don't need your apology. Please leave."

Suddenly, Leticia couldn't see Dwight in the man's eyes anymore. Only a cold color of blue. What kind of man hastily judges a person's character based off of one mistake?

"Fine, I'll leave. Thank you for your understanding."

With that Leticia stormed out of the clinic. How did someone so narrow-minded remind her of Dwight in the first place? He looked at her like she was a mistake of some kind. If she were in his shoes, she would have been offended, but she surely would not dismiss a person that coldly, based on one mistake.

"But what came over you, Letty?" Leticia grumbled as she walked out.

There was no logical explanation as to why she reacted that way. Why attack Oliver instead of Sam who seemed to be the root cause of the problem? Why did she take it out on the doctor? Oliver had every right to be angry, and she needed a reasonable explanation for her actions. It sounded absurd to blame it on his familiar eyes, eyes she'd at first thought were lovely.

Leticia groaned and stared at her palm. The real question was, did she mean to slap Oliver, the doctor? Or Dwight, her deceased love?

CHAPTER EIGHTEEN

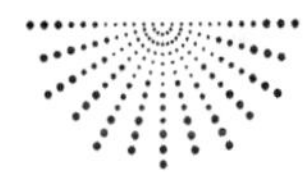

*T*wo *weeks later...*

Margaret paced up and down the hall. She and Carolyn had been sitting in the church pews for a while, waiting for Sherman to finish his counseling session. Thankfully, she had been able to pick up the pieces of her life and decide that she was going to live her days as they came. She wasn't going to think about the future or what it would bring. Instead, she was going to live each day with a positive mindset.

"Maggie, you are going to drill a hole in the floor with your pacing," Carolyn noted. "Sit down."

"I can't. I'm worried."

"I don't get it. I thought you were over this," Carolyn grumbled. "You started working again. You're smiling, at least occasionally. And you're eating. Basically, you're making progress. Now you're back to being worried about Edwin?"

Margaret paused. "Yes."

Carolyn lifted her eyebrows. "The Edwin who broke your heart?"

"Yes."

"The Edwin who said he wanted to marry someone else?"

"Yes."

"The Edwin who wasted your time?"

"Yes."

"The Edwin..."

"Carolyn, stop," Margaret grumbled. "I'm being serious here."

"Well, I'm not. I'm going to be anything but serious about this because as far as I know, you have moved on."

Margaret let out a frustrated sigh. "Can you at least try to support me by keeping an open mind? I begged you to ask Sherman about Edwin but you refused, and now I'm here to do it myself and you're being nonchalant about it."

"I'm being nonchalant because he broke your heart, Maggie. He ripped it right out of your chest and shattered it into a million pieces. I was there, I saw it and I felt the pain. So, forgive me if I think seeking him out is a bad idea."

"Aren't you even going to ask me why I'm looking for him?" Margaret asked, crossing her arms.

"Isn't it obvious? Maggie, I know you. When you see Edwin, you'll melt like butter under the sun. The feelings will return. That's why I think it's a bad idea."

Margaret shrugged her shoulders. "Who says the feelings ever left?"

Carolyn's eyes widened. "Margaret!"

"Even if you don't want to know, I'll tell you the reason anyway," Margaret said. "I think something is going on with Edwin and he's covering it up."

Carolyn shook her head. "I'm not following."

"It's been two weeks," Margaret said. "Edwin hasn't been seen around the town in two weeks and Sam has been working at the clinic every single day."

"All right... I'm still not following."

"For someone he claims to have found a spark with, Edwin sure doesn't visit her at all. And I know this because I may or may not have asked a little boy from the house next to the clinic to find out for me."

Carolyn shook her head. "Really? You had someone spy on Sam and Edwin?"

"Not exactly. But that's how I know that there's something they aren't telling us. And I'm going to find out what it is."

Carolyn bit the inside of her cheek and stared outside through the window. "If that's true, then you do have a point. But if you find out that he lied just to be away from you, what are you going to do then?"

"I'll leave him," Margaret said. "I just can't live without knowing the truth."

That was somewhat of a lie. Margaret had not gotten over Edwin, and she feared that if she saw him again, after so long, she might do something Carolyn would give her an earful for. Margaret had managed to keep the thoughts of Edwin at bay so she could go about her daily life, but the thoughts were still there, and frequently, they popped up. She had no control over them.

Sherman stepped into the room and headed straight for them. "Sorry I kept you both waiting," he apologized.

Margaret sighed in relief and walked over to Sherman's side. She waited for him to say hello to Carolyn before she stood in front of him.

"Sherman, where's Edwin?" Margaret asked. "No one has seen him in two weeks. Now, I know that it shouldn't be my concern since he claims to have found someone else, but I need to know for my own sanity. You just need to tell me where he is. I've checked the boarding house and the rooms here in the church. He isn't here and the only other place he could be is your house."

Sherman glanced at Carolyn and brought his hands to his hips. "Honestly, Margaret, I have no idea. When I noticed that he had been gone for a few days, I got in contact with a couple of the church members who know Edwin, but he isn't with them. Edwin has been practically missing since the night of the dance. I can't find him. About a week ago, I started to do my own digging and I found out that he has not been seen with

Samantha Randall, even though he made claims that night that he was going to marry her."

"Wait, why didn't you tell me that Edwin has gone missing?" Carolyn asked.

"I didn't want to make a big deal out of it until I found him," Sherman said. "I reckoned he was embarrassed, or he felt guilty for what he did, so he went into hiding. But it worries me now because there's nowhere for Edwin to hide for this long." Sherman shrugged his shoulders. "None of this makes sense... and frankly, I'm worried about him."

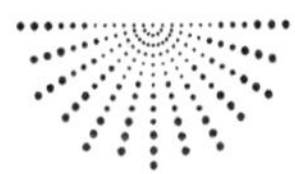

CHAPTER NINETEEN

"The entire situation is strange, it's murky like I can't see the answer for looking," Margaret said. "Something isn't right, Sherman."

"Well, where do you think he'd go?" Carolyn asked. "Somewhere you haven't thought to look."

"How about Samantha herself?" Margaret suggested. "She is Edwin's newly found friend. I think she'll know where he is. She might not say, but she knows something. Remember the night of the dance? She said it wasn't her place to tell."

"Maggie, she could have easily been talking about their relationship," Carolyn said. "I think Sherman is right. Edwin might merely be hiding because he feels guilty and he needs time. Either way, we will find him if that's what you want."

"Find who?"

Leticia's voice startled them. She strolled down the aisle, her gaze set on their faces.

"Oh, no," Margaret said, turning away.

"I told you we should have told her," Carolyn said in a hushed tone. "Now look."

"You know she would have stopped us."

"Tell me what?" Leticia asked, crossing her arms.

It took Margaret a couple of days to summon the courage she needed to ask Carolyn for help on the matter. Margaret knew her friends would be against the idea of her worrying about Edwin. Especially, Leticia, who was the most stubborn one. Margaret feared that Leticia would throw a tantrum if she found out Margaret was still thinking about Edwin. One thing Carolyn and Leticia didn't play with was her happiness.

"You won't lie to me, Sherman," Leticia said turning her eyes on him. "What's going on here?"

Sherman scratched the top of his head and smirked. "Margaret is worried about Edwin and she wants to find him."

"Sherman," Carolyn and Margaret chorused.

Sherman shrugged his shoulders. "You should have told her. It's not fair to keep a friend in the dark."

"What?" Leticia said. "What?"

"I told her not to, Letty," Carolyn said. "I was going to tell you, but Maggie thought…"

"Don't patronize me, Carolyn," Leticia cut her off. She took in a deep breath. "I understand why you didn't tell me. Obviously, I would have locked Margaret in her room if I found out. What were you thinking, Carolyn?"

"I'm not trying to salvage my relationship with him, but hear me out first," Margaret asked.

"Maggie, I know you don't know how to hold grudges, and that's a good thing. But sometimes, you need to let things go. If Edwin doesn't want to be with you, then you shouldn't try to force him to be. Life is like that sometimes, and I really don't want to listen to you cry in the middle of the night. We just got past that stage a few days ago and now you're seeking out the source of your unhappiness again."

"Edwin's missing, Letty," Margaret stated. "No one has seen him in two weeks. That's why I'm worried. Nothing else."

"Missing? More like hiding," Leticia said. "He might have hurt you, but Edwin does have a heart. I'm sure he feels guilty and as such, he doesn't want to show his face around the church."

"It's not just that, Leticia," Sherman chimed in. "Margaret has a valid reason to be worried. Just trust us on this, and let us find Edwin."

Leticia sighed and winked at her friend. "Well, if you got Sherman to believe you, then I suppose we should be worried about Edwin. Just promise me one thing. You will not go back to crying all through the night."

"I won't," Margaret assured her.

"Good, so, what's the plan?" Leticia asked.

"Well, we're heading to the Doc's to speak to Sam. We're sure she knows something, and we are going to try and get her to talk to us."

Leticia raised her eyebrows. "The Doc's? Awesome."

"What's wrong?"

"Nothing. I just won't follow you inside," Leticia mumbled. "Shall we?"

Margaret let out a sigh of relief. It was much easier to convince Leticia to hop on board the plan than she thought it would be. Margaret understood that they were only looking out for her wellbeing, but she couldn't bring herself to tell them that she couldn't shake off the feeling that Edwin needed her.

After she had spent days crying, she began to reminisce about the time she had spent with him. Strangely, the Edwin she felt an instant connection with when they first met, and the Edwin she saw for the last time at the town dance, were the same person, only that the latter seemed depressed. Margaret thought that Edwin had changed overnight, but she couldn't bring herself to believe it. It was then she thought that perhaps, Edwin did not change. Something changed in him.

Whatever it was, she was going to find it out. Even if her relationship with Edwin had ended forever, Margaret needed closure. She couldn't move on without it.

"Maggie, if we happen to find Edwin, are you sure you're ready to see him again?" Leticia asked.

"It won't be a big deal, Letty," Margaret lied. "I just need to get to the bottom of this situation. My heart keeps telling me that this isn't the Edwin I know."

Leticia glanced at her. "You know, Carolyn and I don't hate Edwin necessarily. We just don't like that he hurt you. And we won't forgive him without a reasonable explanation."

"I know," Margaret said softly. "That's why I love you both so much. You take on my fight like it's yours. I'm never alone."

"You would do the same for us, Maggie. Right from the start, all you wanted was for the three of us to be happy. The path might be rough, but we're still on the right track."

"I'm sorry I didn't tell you, Letty. I thought you would stop me."

"Oh, I would have," Leticia replied. "But seeing that everyone else agrees with you, I think we should get to the bottom of this and sort it out once and for all."

Margaret nodded and inhaled nervously as they approached the clinic. She hadn't figured out what she was going to say to Samantha when she saw her. Margaret still didn't know how she felt about the lady.

She hesitated at the door. There was talking inside and she could hear it as plain as day. With her hand on the handle, she froze.

"I don't know what we can do for him because he is already losing his sight at this point..." Samantha said from behind the door. "He is going blind for sure. But Edwin doesn't want to talk about it."

Margaret took a step back. Perhaps she didn't hear correctly. Who was losing what?

CHAPTER TWENTY

"What did you just say, Samantha?" Margaret said as she pushed open the door and walked in.

Margaret could barely hear herself talk. She wasn't sure if the others could hear her either. Her heart was beating so fast in her chest that the drumming took over her hearing. What in the world had happened to Edwin?

Oliver and Samantha stared at them like they were looking at ghosts. They glanced at each other, exchanging knowing looks.

"Edwin is here, isn't he?" Carolyn asked. "Of course. Where else would he be?"

"He's not," Samantha answered but she lowered her eyes and color flooded her cheeks.

Margaret took a step forward. "What did you say about Edwin? What are the both of you hiding that you think you need to protect so badly? You might think you know Edwin and you are only protecting his interest, but you have known him only a few weeks. Sherman here has known him for years and he is practically family. Do you think it's fair that you're keeping us in the dark like this? You know something, but you refuse to tell."

"I wanted to tell you," Samantha said. "In fact, I tried to encourage Edwin to tell you all because he needs people who care about him now more than ever. But Edwin insisted that it was for the best and as I said before, it was not my place to tell."

"Well, since we already heard you say something that shocking, you might as well tell us," Carolyn said. "What did you mean?"

Samantha turned to her father, and when he nodded, she nodded too. "Edwin is going blind. In fact, right now, he has lost his ability to see. He can only see shapes now, and shadows clearly. His vision is blurry, and soon the shapes and the shadows are all he will be able to see, shortly after that he will see nothing."

Margaret found it hard to close her mouth. "What? I don't understand."

She didn't want to understand. Instead, she hoped that there was something wrong with her hearing and she was imagining things.

"What, do you mean, blind?" Sherman asked. "What happened to him? How can a healthy man just lose his sight?"

"It's something that runs in his family. It starts with heavy eyes, but Edwin didn't know about the symptoms, so when his eyes felt heavy, he thought he was just tired or sleepy. But when I asked him about his other symptoms, I was able to piece together the clues. For one, the first time I saw him, it took a while for him to focus on my face. His gaze was... darting all about and then I sensed it. He kept squinting like he was trying hard to see me. Edwin didn't think much of it, because he didn't know. When he found out, it shattered him. His world literally came crashing down."

Margaret slumped on the chair. "Why didn't he say anything to us?"

"He didn't want to burden you, Margaret," Samantha said. "Nothing is going on between the two of us. In fact, we were barely friends that day at the dance. When I diagnosed him, I told him I was going to do some more reading. So, when he saw me at the dance, I signaled to him that I had some information. I had to tell him that he only had weeks before his sight was completely gone and I needed him to brace himself for it. He was devastated by the news, so I hugged him... to console him. That was when you saw us, and the whole thing escalated. He didn't want you to spend the rest of your life tending to a blind man when you could find happiness with someone else." Samantha stopped to let them take it all in but everyone was too stunned to speak and so she continued.

"I was all right with being the enemy as he found solace in his condition. These types of things tend to drive people insane. One minute you're fine, and the next day, you wake up blind. He really needed to prepare his mind for it and if that was the way he chose to do it, then I couldn't stop him... even though I wanted to... he needs his friends around him, and yet, he has pushed them all away."

"You are right, that makes no sense," Carolyn rasped. "A man needs his family, especially when he is going through something so life-changing. He needs support. During the war, do you know how many soldiers on their dying beds begged to see their families one last time? I can understand the part about Edwin not wanting to burden anyone, but you should know better as a doctor. He needs his friends, whether he would like to admit it or not."

"Sam knows that," Oliver said. "That's what she's trying to say. She tried to explain it to Edwin, but he was adamant that he wanted to be alone with his condition. He didn't want to inconvenience anyone with his plight."

Sherman scoffed. "Typical. He always kept things like that to himself. But when did he start to think of himself as an inconvenience?"

"Understand it from his perspective," Samantha said. "I know you're offended that he chose to fight this battle himself, but Edwin was sure that if the truth came out... that Margaret would understand that he did it with everyone's best interest at heart."

"I don't understand," Margaret said, then sighed. "Where is he, Sam?"

Samantha fiddled with her fingers. "I promised Edwin I wouldn't tell anyone his whereabouts."

The silence was heavy in the room. Margaret wanted to shout, to scream that it wasn't fair but she felt so weak that she also wanted to curl into a corner and cry. How could she help him if he wouldn't let her?

CHAPTER TWENTY-ONE

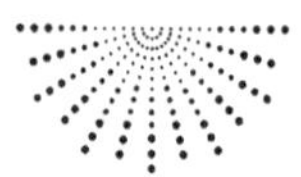

argaret knew she had to find out where Edwin was; she would help him, they all would.

"Well, I didn't make any promise," Oliver said. "And I agree with them on this. Edwin needs them. If he refuses to talk to us about how he is feeling, maybe, he'll talk to her. He's in the cottage behind my house. He has been there for two weeks. He barely eats, talks, or leaves his bed. I'll take you."

"Thank you, Doctor Randall," Margaret said, rising to her feet.

Oliver led her through the back door and they walked past the main house, making their way to the cottage at the far end of the property. Mixed emotions coursed through Margaret. She was angry that he hadn't confided in her, sad that he was going through this all alone, and relieved that he was safe somewhere.

Oliver unlocked the door from outside and ushered Margaret in. She thanked him again and waited until he shut the door before she proceeded into the room. A tear dropped to her cheeks when she saw Edwin seated by the window with his eyes closed. She walked over to him quietly and squatted by his side.

"Sam?" Edwin said with a cracked voice.

"Not Sam. Margaret."

Edwin's eyes flung wide open but he didn't meet her gaze.

It took him a while, but his eyes found her. "Maggie? What are you doing here?"

"What are you doing here, Edwin?" Margaret asked. "Did you really think this was going to change things between us?"

Edwin's lips quivered and he looked away, a poor attempt to hide the tears welling up in his eyes.

Margaret touched his face with her palm. "We have been through a lot in the short time that we've been together. What were you thinking... keeping your condition to yourself? Did you think you were doing me a favor?"

"I don't want you taking on the responsibility, Maggie," Edwin said with a trembling voice. "It's not fair to you."

"Let me decide what's fair to me and what's not. Don't you trust me, Edwin? Don't you trust that I would help you? Did you think I'd abandon you?"

Edwin shook his head. "I knew you'd stay. But I don't want you to. I don't want you to suffer because of me."

"I wish you would have been honest with me. I love you, Edwin. I want to be with you no matter what."

Her words caused Edwin to shudder. "Maggie..."

He jerked, kicking a table by the side of the window that had a lantern on it. Usually, Sam came in every morning to put out the lantern Edwin used during the night, but she hadn't come to see him that morning. The lantern fell and immediately broke. The flame quickly caught the rug, and then the curtains and in the blink of an eye, there was an out-of-control fire.

Margaret screamed and sprung to her feet.

"Is that fire?" Edwin asked, staggering to his feet. "Maggie, go. Go outside, now."

"Not without you," she protested. "You can barely see."

The heat was getting unbearable and Margaret was paralyzed by how fast the fire grew.

"I'll be behind you," Edwin said. "Go."

"Given the type of person you are, you might just sit back down after I leave," Margaret said. "Not a chance. Put your arm over my shoulder. I'll guide you."

"Margaret, I'll only slow you down."

"Shut up, Edwin, and let me save you," Margaret yelled, scared to bits. "Goodness! We go together or not at all."

Margaret threw Edwin's arm over her shoulder and began to cautiously walk on the hot rug, trying to find her way to the door. She could barely see a thing with all the smoke in the room, but she relied on her senses to guide her to the door. Edwin could barely walk. His knees buckled with every few steps he took. He was weak, perhaps because he was starving himself.

To their rescue, Oliver came bursting through the door. He took Edwin from her and led them outside quickly. They crashed onto the ground just outside the cottage, trying to get some fresh air.

"What happened?" Oliver asked.

"The lantern fell and the flames caught the curtain," Margaret explained.

Sherman, Carolyn, and Samantha rushed toward them with buckets of water in a bid to douse the flaming house.

"I'm so sorry," Edwin said, leaning against the wall. "It's my fault. I hit the table and the lantern fell. I didn't know it was on or else I would have put it off at the break of dawn. I'm sorry, Oliver."

"Oh, it's all right. The cottage can always be repaired. I'm just glad that you and Margaret are in one piece. It could have been a lot worse. Thankfully, you're both fine."

"Margaret, are you all right?" Leticia asked, rushing to her side. "I heard the ruckus and I came over to check. Did you hurt yourself?"

Margaret shook her head. "I'm perfectly fine."

Edwin chuckled but his smile slowly waned. He clasped his head with one hand and reached for Margaret's with the other. Edwin held on to it firmly as his head spun in circles.

"Edwin, are you all right?" Oliver asked. "Is it another dizzy spell?"

"Yes," Edwin whispered before crashing into Margaret's arms.

CHAPTER TWENTY-TWO

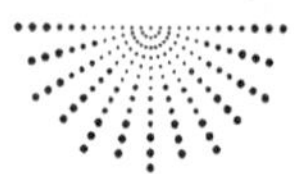

Margaret groaned and straightened her back. The air was chilly that morning and a cold draft had woken her up. She had fallen asleep sitting on a chair by Edwin's side. He had moved back to his boarding house since there was no use hiding anymore.

Edwin had apologized for keeping his condition to himself, but he explained that it was the only solution he could think of.

They had barely spoken to each other since they arrived at the boarding house the day before. Edwin really wanted to speak, but he was too tired to make a complete sentence, and although Margaret had a lot she wanted to say too, she decided to let him be. She had fallen asleep watching him.

A soft knock on the door snapped Margaret back to reality. She hastily rose to her feet in a bid to open the door before the knocking woke Edwin up. Margaret slowly unlocked the door and with a smile, she ushered Sherman and Samantha into the room.

"How is he?" Sherman asked, almost in a whisper.

"I don't know yet, he hasn't woken up."

"Samantha wanted to come and check up on him to make sure that he was all right after the fire," Sherman explained. "That's why I brought her along."

"Please, go ahead," Margaret said to Samantha, stepping aside.

Sherman and Margaret stood in the corner of the room and watched Samantha unlock her small box. Margaret had to apologize to Samantha soon. Not only for her attitude towards her but also for the untoward things she had thought of doing to Samantha when she still misunderstood the situation.

"You know, Edwin used to talk about his blind parents occasionally," Sherman started. "They died when he was twelve."

Margaret stared at Sherman. "Do you know how they passed away?"

"Pneumonia," Sherman answered. "He always said that period was traumatizing for him. Watching them suffer, when he couldn't do much at his young age. He took care of them for a year after they went blind and when they died, something in him broke. He preferred to be alone, so he ran away from the orphanage, and he stayed by himself for a while."

"You changed that about him," Margaret told him. "He was glad that he found you. Deep down, I don't think Edwin really wanted to be alone. He just didn't think he'd find someone like you."

"His blindness must have reminded him of that period in his life when he felt truly alone," Sherman stated.

"I'm not leaving his side. We are going to figure this out together. His days of handling things alone are over. Whether he likes it or not." Margaret managed a smile.

Samantha rose to her feet and walked over to their side. "He'll be all right. Please make sure he eats something when he wakes up. It'll give him strength. He's blind, not bedridden. Don't let him have his way, Margaret. Remind him that it is not the end of the world."

Margaret nodded. "Thank you, Sam," she said with a faint smile. "I should also apologize for misjudging you. All you were trying to do was help. You didn't deserve to take the blame for this."

"All is forgotten," Samantha said. "I understand. I would have hated me too."

"Thanks for your support and thank you for taking care of him," Margaret said.

"You're welcome," she answered. "I'll take my leave now. If there's anything else, please do not hesitate to send for me."

"I won't."

"I'll be going too," Sherman said. "I'll be back with Carolyn later in the day to see him. Do you need anything?"

Margaret paused to think, then gently shook her head. "No, I can handle things. Thank you, Sherman."

Once they left, Margaret shut the door and returned to Edwin's side. She checked to see if he was still sound asleep before lying down on the other side of the bed. She had seen soldiers lose their sight during the war. Most of the time, it happened suddenly, due to a blast or a gunshot. It was strange how they braced themselves for death during the war, but then losing their sight seemed more painful than dying. The thought of living in darkness for the rest of their lives drove them to the edge.

"Maggie?" Edwin moaned and stirred in his sleep. "Maggie?"

It was progress. At least he wasn't calling out for his doctor in his sleep. "I'm here. I'm right beside you," she whispered.

Edwin slowly opened his eyes but kept them lowered. "You didn't leave."

"I'm not leaving," she whispered. "But I'm still a bit angry at you."

"Only a bit?"

"Yes, only a bit. Because a part of me understands, but the other part of me is angry that you pushed me away in the cruelest way possible."

"I'm sorry, but that was the only way to get you to forget me."

"Well, it didn't work," Margaret said. "You should have told me. Your condition doesn't change our relationship. We only need to adapt."

Edwin lifted his eyes, following the sound of her voice. With his finger, he traced her face, touching her chin, her lips, her nose, and then her eyes."

"I can't see you, Maggie." Edwin's voice quivered. "It's so dark, I'm not sure if it's day or night. I don't know if your hair is tied up as you prefer, or if you left it to fall on your shoulders like I prefer. I don't know if you've been crying, because I can't see your eyes. I will never see you again, Maggie."

Margaret moved closer to him. "It's morning. My hair isn't tied up, and I have not been crying. At least, not in the last five days. I can tell you whatever it is you want to know. As I said, we will adapt."

"You once told me how you working as a nurse during the war was traumatizing for you. That you and your friends were not thinking about working as nurses anymore because you wanted to move on from that life and forget all the pain that came with watching people die. You shouldn't have to compromise your happiness for me. You deserve so much better, Maggie. Someone who can see you, and remind you every day that you are beautiful and that you deserve the world. I don't want you living like a nurse any longer, and if you're with me, that's what you will be."

"Well, I wasn't in love during the war," Margaret said. "And, I wasn't happy. I love you, Edwin. That changes everything. I am happy with you, and if I'm not with you, I don't feel complete. If we can no longer stare at each another, we can rely on touch, we can still kiss, we can have picnics, and you don't need to see me before you tell me how beautiful you think I am."

"You really feel this way?" Edwin asked. "Because if you don't leave me right now... if you choose to stay, I can never let you go again."

Margaret leaned in and placed her head on his chest. "I was the one who made Carolyn and Leticia move from New Hampshire to Appleton. We came West in search of something better. In search of happiness. I was broken, deceived, my feelings were hurt along the way, and sometimes, I wondered if I was enough."

"You are enough."

Margaret smiled. "Then I met you and I started hearing things like that from someone who wasn't Carolyn or Leticia. That day when we met, I was heartbroken because Carolyn was trying to sacrifice her happiness for us to flee. As I scurried to the wagon, you were sitting there with this serious stare on your face. Then our eyes locked, and your gaze softened. You smiled at me, and you didn't take your eyes off of me for the longest time. Your gaze was different from the ones I received working at the saloon. It was innocent. I didn't tell you this back then, but it made me feel special. My point is, I am not going to throw that away so easily."

"All I wanted to do was make you happy. Now, I am not so confident that I can do that. I had so much planned. It's depressing just thinking about it."

Margaret tilted her head upwards and ran her fingers through Edwin's hair. She planted a kiss on his lips and gazed into his eyes. "I will always look at you with nothing but love, Edwin."

"Will you'll tell me everything?" Edwin asked. "You will tell me when you are sad, or happy, or when something is bothering you? I won't know, Margaret, and I want to know. I still want to try to be the man you deserve, but I need your help too. Samantha said it's possible to know these things by just listening to your voice and how you speak. She said it'll take time, but it's possible. So, while I learn to read your emotions in other ways, tell me everything."

"I promise," Margaret answered. "But the same goes for you too. Don't keep your needs bottled up inside. Talk to me, Edwin. I don't like it when you hide things from me. To be honest, if you can keep something this life-changing to yourself, I wonder if you will keep doing it. Talk to me."

Edwin placed his hand on her cheek and lowered his head. "I promise. I won't hide anything from you."

Edwin returned her kiss and caressed her cheek with his fingers. "I love you, Maggie. I'll be good to you, I promise."

Margaret wrapped her arm around him. "We'll adapt. Don't worry."

"You know we have a rough journey ahead of us," Edwin said. "Can I provide for us? How can I ask you to give up so much for me?"

"We'll adapt, Edwin," Margaret repeated with a smile. "We'll make the journey interesting and I'm gaining love."

Edwin tightened his arms around her and kissed her on the forehead. Margaret hoped to God that she had finally been able to convince him that it wasn't the end of the world. Once he got used to his condition, things were bound to get better. But the rough journey he talked about was just beginning. Still, Margaret found herself excited about the future. Things were perfect. They weren't the way she thought they would be, but as long as she was with Edwin, they could accomplish anything.

"Would you like something to eat?" Margaret asked him. "You have to eat."

"Yes," Edwin said. "I'm starving."

CHAPTER TWENTY-THREE

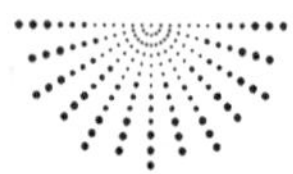

"I sort of don't know how to feel about Edwin right now," Leticia said, with her wrists deep in soapy water.

Carolyn giggled at her statement. "It was all a misunderstanding. You can let go of your grudges against him now."

"I know, I know," Leticia said. "But he still hurt Maggie trying to protect her. I don't know how that makes me feel. Margaret cried a lot because of him."

"I was there, I saw her. But I also know that Maggie really wants to be with Edwin. Who are we to stop her from finding happiness? Wasn't that the reason we moved in the first place?"

"You're right," Leticia said.

"Now, you're the only one that's left to let go of your past, and find happiness." Carolyn smiled.

Leticia dropped the cloth in her hand back into the soapy water and stared at Carolyn. "And who told you I haven't found happiness?"

"Letty, come on."

"What? For all you know, I am perfectly happy with how my life is right now. I have work and I have you both. What more do I have to ask for?"

"A family," Carolyn said. "Love."

"That will come at the right time. When it's time for it to happen, it'll happen. I don't have to force it. Take you and Sherman for instance. You met him by accident, and now he is the most important person in your life. I personally have no idea how Margaret and Edwin happened, but it did. No one can compete with fate. Whatever will be, will be and I'm fine with that."

Carolyn gazed at Leticia, proud of how her mindset about life had changed. After Dwight's death, they didn't think Leticia was ever going to open up her heart to anyone ever again, but now, here, there seemed to be hope.

"What?" Leticia asked Carolyn. "Why are you staring at me that way?"

"I just didn't think you'd open your heart to new possibilities," Carolyn said. "Losing Dwight was so devastating for you, and you shut your heart to everything. In fact, you were convinced that you were never going to get over his death. I'm glad to hear you talk about fate and possibilities."

"Oh, well." Leticia sighed. "I guess my heart yearns for what you have. But I also know that I'm not over Dwight, so I don't want to rush it."

"Baby steps," Carolyn said with a proud look in her eyes. "We'll get there."

"Do you still worry about the possibility of Porter finding us?" Leticia asked her.

Carolyn paused to think. "After my conversation with Sherman about it, I have worried less. Sherman is convinced that Porter is occupied somewhere far from here with another devious plan. One that doesn't concern us. If Sherman says not to worry, then I'm not worried."

"I'm not worried either," Leticia said. "It took a while before we found this town. There are numerous towns in South Dakota, and I don't think Porter or Brandon will devote all their time to finding us. I'm just happy we got away from them in one piece."

"But there's one thing I want to confess," Carolyn said. "Whenever I think of Brandon, and how he almost ruined my life, my blood chills. I can't explain how I feel, because it's sort of a mixture of different emotions. There's anger, fear, resentment, and pity, all wrapped up in one bundle. I never want to see the face of that man again."

"Neither do I. They almost ruined us. I'll never get over it."

Carolyn picked up the dress she had dropped into the water and continued to wash it. Thanks to Sherman, she had learned to worry less about things she could not change. Her perspective on life had changed for the better since she arrived in Appleton and her worrying had decreased significantly, partially because there was not a lot to worry about.

"Carolyn, Sherman is here to see you," Penny announced, poking her head out from the passageway.

"Oh, he's here for their afternoon walk," Leticia teased. "How utterly romantic."

Carolyn quickly rinsed her hands and scurried to the front of the restaurant where Sherman was waiting patiently for her. His face lit up in delight when he saw her running up to him. Carolyn stopped right in front of him, smiling and panting at the same time.

Sherman smiled back. "Good afternoon, Carolyn. I see you took your time to come to me."

"Don't tease me," Carolyn breathed.

"Why'd you run? I was already waiting for you, so you might as well have taken your time. Now you're out of breath."

"It doesn't matter. I'm here now."

Sherman offered her his arm. "Shall we?"

They walked down the path, heading nowhere in particular. Sometimes, during their routine walks, they would stop and sit by a tree, to enjoy the nice scenery or to talk about something more serious than their normal chitchat. Carolyn loved their walks.

"How's Edwin?" Carolyn asked him. "Did you visit him at the boarding house today?"

Sherman nodded. "I did. He is much better now. Margaret is teaching him how to walk around the room by himself. She says that he bumped into the chair one time when he wanted to use the bathroom so she felt the need."

"That's sweet," Carolyn noted. "They are going to be really busy for the next couple of weeks. Knowing the kind of person Edwin is, he would probably want Margaret to teach him everything he could do by himself. I'm just glad that they are happy together."

"Me too. Samantha says that soon, he will lose his eyesight completely. I don't know how to feel about that. I feel bad for Edwin, but I know he'll get through this and come out victorious."

"I hope he does," Carolyn said.

"Carolyn, I know a lot has been going on, but have you given my proposal any thought?" Sherman asked. "We didn't get to finish our discussion that day."

Carolyn inhaled deeply. "I have given it some thought." She lowered her eyes, avoiding his gaze.
The smile dropped off Sherman's face and was replaced with worry.

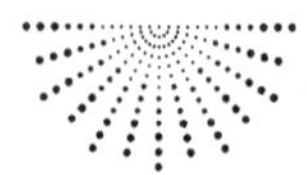

CHAPTER TWENTY-FOUR

Sherman stopped in his tracks and stood facing her. "So, tell me. What do you say? Do you accept my proposal, Carolyn? I love you so much. Will you marry me?"

Carolyn took Sherman's hands into hers and squeezed them. "You know, I thought I was married once... to Brandon. Leticia and I were just talking about it before you arrived. Just thinking about the fact that I was walking down the aisle and I had to hold Brandon's hand and say the words, 'I do', to him makes my skin crawl. Thankfully, it was a faux, and I escaped that, but I still think about it from time to time. But that is the past." She had kept her face serious and could see that he was worried. She couldn't torture him anymore. "The answer is yes, I cannot wait to walk down the aisle for real, and say 'I do', to the man I truly love."

Sherman raised his eyebrow and a smile formed on his face. He dropped down to one knee and pulled out the ring from his pocket. "Carolyn Darby, will you make me the happiest man on the face of the Earth and marry me?"

"Yes, Sherman. It would be an honor to be called your wife." Carolyn beamed her brightest smile.

Sherman slipped the ring onto her finger and lifted Carolyn off the ground. He twirled with her in his arms before setting her down and giving her a warm hug.

"I promise, I will do my best to make you forget all about Brandon and what he did to you," Sherman said, holding her in his arms.

"You don't have to try so hard," Carolyn said before taking a step back. "You know, on that day in question, when I was standing in front of Brandon, listening to that man read the vows, I was thinking of you. At first, I stared at the door, hoping you would burst through it in shining armor, riding on a white horse. Then later on, as I was forced to say 'I do', I imagined you standing there, not Brandon. I said 'I do' to the image of you in my head.

It might sound weird, but I think God heard my prayers that day, that's why he let our paths cross once again."

Sherman stroked her cheek. "I was sure of my intentions with you from the very first day. Well, I was sure that I wanted to be involved in your life, I just didn't know how. You keep saying that I saved you, but have you thought about how you saved me?"

Carolyn's eyebrows furrowed. "I saved you?"

Sherman nodded. "The idea of falling in love with someone was foreign to me before you came along. I didn't think I'd find someone that would ignite the spark in my heart the way that you did. After that day, when we first met, I could not stop thinking about you. It started then, and I am glad we didn't lose each other."

"I love you, Sherman. I really do and that's not going to change," Carolyn confessed.

"I love you too, Carolyn."

They held hands as they continued their stroll down the path, talking about Minnesota and the time they shared together there. Carolyn had learned to compartmentalize her worry. She could hear that little voice in her head, telling her all of the things that could go wrong, how she was on the verge of ruining Sherman's reputation and jeopardizing what he built there in Appleton. But she didn't listen to any of it. If Sherman was sure about marrying her, even with her past, nothing else mattered.

"I don't want you worrying about anything," Sherman said as if he read her mind. "It's completely fine to have worries but don't let it cloud your reasoning. We are in this together, Carolyn. I'll protect you to the very best of my abilities. So, put your trust in me."

"I'm not worried, Sherman," she lied. "I trust you. And I've prayed about the fears I have. I know that at the end of everything, things will turn out fine. I'm not bothered."

"When did you get so optimistic?" Sherman asked. "Usually, Margaret is the optimistic one."

Carolyn laughed. "What? How do you know that?"

"I've been around the three of you long enough to study your characters. You three are different sides of one whole. You match each other perfectly."

"All right. So, if Margaret is the optimistic one, then what am I?"

Sherman inhaled sharply. "You are the level-headed one in the group. Like the mother, with two children. They are both guided by you, they both listen to you... well, you all listen to each other but... they listen to you more. You worry quite a lot, you take your time making decisions to not make a mistake, and most of the time you make good choices but occasionally you make the worst choices. Like with Brandon and how you thought you were saving your friends by being a hero, forgetting that your friends in question are pretty stubborn women too."

"Ouch." Carolyn giggled. "I guess you know me too well. What about Leticia?"

"Leticia..." Sherman paused to think. "She is impulsive. The most stubborn one amongst you three and brave. I still recall what she did in the forest. It takes a lot of courage to charge a man with a gun. She not only did that, but she scared them off with it too. She has a strong will, and she hardly ever forgets."

"She actually doesn't ever forget things," Carolyn said. "I just hope that she can try to forget some of her pain, so she can move on with her life."

"She has you and Margaret to help her with that," Sherman said. "She'll be fine. You all will be fine. You've gone through too much not to be."

"Thank you, Sherman."

Carolyn leaned into him. She and Sherman were about to start a future together. One she had not thought possible. Sherman loved her. He didn't need to say it for her to be sure of it. The way he talked, the look in his eyes, and his actions spoke loud enough.

"So, what's next for us?" Carolyn asked, staring at the man who completed her life.

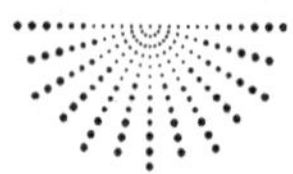

CHAPTER TWENTY-FIVE

"Congratulations on your engagement!" a couple who'd just walked into the hall told Carolyn.

"Thank you so much, and thank you for coming. Have fun!" Leticia mouthed at the same time that Carolyn said those words to the couple.

Leticia could hardly hold back her smile as she watched her friend struggle to keep up with the crowd. It was the best time to tease her about it, but she decided to keep her jokes until later. Carolyn was already exhausted. Sherman had informed her he would be throwing an engagement dance to celebrate taking their relationship to the next step, but it was obvious she hadn't expected him to invite the entire community. It was like the town dance all over again. Carolyn had been congratulated so many times, that it was starting to sound like a chant.

"Letty, there have got to be about a hundred people here," Carolyn said, amazed. "It's not even my wedding day."

"Imagine what that is going to look like," Leticia said.

"He said a small betrothal celebration. When he said small, I thought maybe the church staff and a few other people, but this is the entire community."

"It's not," Leticia countered. "But it's a lot. And stop whining. You should be happy that there are this many people here to congratulate you. Sherman is a popular man in this town. Everyone loves him."

"Yes, but he loves me more," Carolyn bragged, flipping her hair dramatically.

Leticia scoffed. "Obviously. But that's not the point. The point is, be happy you have this crowd. How many people showed up at your last wedding?"

It slipped. Leticia had promised herself she would keep the jokes until after the ceremony when Carolyn was more at ease, but she let one slip and in return, she got a death stare from her best friend.

"I love you," Leticia said, laughing awkwardly. "I'm sorry."

"I doubt that." Carolyn smacked her on the arm. "Don't tease me about things like that. Besides, it wasn't a real wedding so it doesn't count. And if you are so eager to know... there were four people present."

Leticia loved how Carolyn had learned to make jokes about their past. She wasn't as uptight about it as she was before. Leticia knew that it was thanks to Sherman, and for that she was grateful. Joking about their ordeal lessened the impact it had on them. If they could laugh about it, then its hold on their lives decreased.

"I'm sorry, it slipped out. I was going to save the jokes until later."

Another older couple walked up to them. "Congratulations on your betrothal, Carolyn."

"Thank you so much, and thank you for coming. Have fun!" Leticia answered in Carolyn's stead.

"Thank you so much, Mr. and Mrs. Anthony. Please enjoy the rest of the evening," Carolyn said. She then turned back to Leticia and shot her a glare. "Stop teasing me."

"I really won't," Leticia answered. "But I'm happy for you, and I love this dance. It's the same set of fiddlers that are playing. I remember being so mesmerized by their music the last time that I didn't even realize you both had left me."

Carolyn giggled. "Every time I imagine that in my head, I cannot help but laugh. I see you dancing in the hall, twirling all by yourself, and then in the next scene, all I'm seeing is Margaret sobbing and accosting Edwin for betraying her. You were so oblivious to what was going on that day."

Leticia chuckled lightly. That was exactly the scenario that played out that day. Leticia remembered how much she loved the slow tune the fiddlers were playing. She'd loved it so much that she'd decided to seek out Margaret to ask her to dance with her. All of that was going on at the same time that Edwin was breaking Margaret's heart.

"Now that you and Maggie are going to start building homes, I'll be more alone than ever," Leticia remarked. "I am happy and sad at the same time."

"You're never going to be alone, Letty. Remember that Maggie and I cannot possibly live without you. We can't live without each other. Just like that time I tried to marry Brandon for your freedom and you came back. That's how it's always going to be between us. We're inseparable."

Carolyn had no idea how much Leticia really needed to hear those words. She was scared to be alone, especially when she had dreams of Dwight again. The dreams had started to frustrate and scare Leticia so much that she sometimes didn't want to sleep at night. It was tormenting, and she had no idea what to do about it.

"You're thinking about the dreams again, aren't you?"

Leticia nodded. "I don't think it has anything to do with my love for him, Carolyn. I loved Dwight, but my heart had wrapped its head around the fact that he is no more, so it doesn't ache anymore when I think of him. Then I have these dreams and I wake up in a cold sweat. I hate seeing his dead body, Carolyn. I hate it so much. Why can't I just hold on to the good part of these dreams? Why does it have to torment me? I'm not holding on to Dwight, but it's like my brain has a mind of its own."

Carolyn made to speak when she felt someone poke her from the back. She jumped and spun around to find Margaret giggling, proud of her little gimmick.

Leticia smiled softly. That was the Maggie she knew. The cheerful one with sparkling blue eyes and a killer smile.

"Hello, girls," Margaret beamed. "I've been looking all over for you both."

"Where's Edwin?" Leticia asked her. "Did you leave him alone?"

Margaret nodded. "He can handle himself. We spent the last week walking and mapping out the church, so he knows his way around this place. And a lot of people are so eager to help him. Edwin likes and hates it, but he has no choice but to accept their help when they offer it. Plus, if he needs me, he will just send someone to call me."

"I'm proud of him," Carolyn said.

Edwin had gone completely blind. When they broke the news to them that he couldn't see anything, not even shapes and shadows, they were all devastated. Leticia had still held on to her grudge against him for what he did to Margaret, but it dissipated because she finally understood him. Margaret was working hard to help him, and that was exactly what he was avoiding. He tried to push her away for her own good. So, she didn't spend the rest of her life with a blind man. But what he didn't know was that Margaret was a stubborn one.

"I'm proud of him too," Leticia added. "And you too, Margaret."

"Thank you," Margaret answered. "So, Leticia, you're the only one that's left to…"

"All right, let's not talk about me right now. It's Carolyn's engagement day. Let's dwell on that," Leticia said.

Carolyn and Margaret exchanged knowing looks. "You will find your own man, whether you want to, or not," Margaret assured her. "I'll sit on your neck if that's what it would take to make you put yourself out there."

"And what makes you think that I haven't put myself out there?"

"Oh, please." Carolyn scoffed. "You've turned down three men this evening, Letty. Three men who politely asked to dance with you. Do you need us to list the things you do or how you go out of your way to avoid conversations with people of the male gender?"

"Like I said," Leticia stuttered. "It's Carolyn's engagement day. Let's focus on her."

Margaret shook her head. "I need to get back to Edwin. I'll see you both later?"

"See you," Leticia said.

"I'll go see what Sherman's doing," Carolyn said. "Letty, please dance with at least one person tonight. It's all I ask. Please."

"Fine," Leticia whined. "Go on now."

Leticia watched her friends hurry away in different directions, leaving her standing there alone. She smiled to herself, proud of the progress they had made since they stopped being nurses after the war. Things were starting to look up. Perhaps not for her, but for her friends. And Leticia was content with that. She didn't need a man, she told herself and pushed down the feeling of dread and emptiness that threatened to overwhelm her.

* * *

Margaret felt a big smile cross her face as she joined Edwin.

"I can tell you are smiling," he said.

"What me, how did you know it was me?" she asked.

"I can recognize your walk. Take my arm." He held out his right arm, a stick was in his left to stop him from walking into things.

Margaret took it, feeling a warm spark travel up to her heart. "Are you okay, is there anything you need? Do you want to go home?"

"I'm fine. I wish I could dance with you."

There was a slight smile on his face but also a touch of something that tugged at her heart. He still felt that he was not enough for her and she knew that she had to show him that he was. Their love for each other was not in doubt, but he had to know that he was all she needed.

"You can," she said and pulled him into her arms. Gently, she took the stick and leaned it against the wall. They were to one side and the area around them was clear. "Hold onto me and let the music take you."

It felt wonderful to be in his arms and although they were doing little but rocking together in time to the music, it filled her with joy.

"We are dancing," he said, a note of delight in his voice. "It feels so good to hold you."

"I feel the same, I feel safe and cherished in your arms."

"I will always cherish you, my love," he said. "However, I'm not sure that our dancing is very stylish."

Margaret chuckled against his neck. It felt so wonderful to be in his arms and she would not swap this moment for the world. "If you remember, our dancing was never that stylish; I guess little has changed."

Edwin chuckled and the sound and feel of it filled her with joy. They had each other and they had the best of friends, they could do this. It felt at that moment as if they were meant for this very moment as if it was the culmination of some grand plan. Maybe, the Lord had tested them, but if He had, the rewards were great. She had Edwin to love and to hold, what more could she ask for?

"I love you so much and I will do everything I can to be worthy," he whispered into her ear.

"You are more than worthy, my love," she said and relaxed against his shoulder enjoying the dancing as the fiddlers continued to play. It was then that she realized that Edwin had never thought of her as fat. All he had ever seen was the true her and that was worth so much, her confidence was back and she was stronger than ever.

CHAPTER TWENTY-SIX

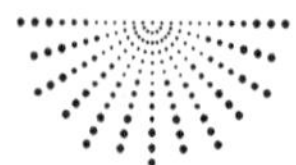

As she made to turn around, Leticia bumped into a tall man. She staggered back and lifted her head to apologize when her eyes fell on Oliver. Her heart raced into a hurried gallop, and she was suddenly breathing hard.

Leticia covered her mouth and coughed. She had not spoken to Oliver after the... incident.

"Are you all right?" Oliver asked her.

"Perfect," Leticia blurted out. "Thank you."

Oliver nodded and made to walk past her but Leticia stood in his path. "Wait a minute," she stammered. "We have unfinished business."

Oliver stopped and faced her again. "We do, don't we?"

"We do." Leticia cleared her throat. "You didn't have to be so rude the other day, you know. I know I might have overreacted, but you were over the top judging me based off of one mistake I made."

Oliver raised his eyebrows. "I was the one that was... over the top?"

"Well, no, but... I guess I just wanted to properly apologize," Leticia said. "I shouldn't have slapped you across the face just because I thought you were having an affair with another woman."

"Another woman?"

"Sorry, the same woman... I mean, Sam. You know what I mean," Leticia stuttered. "I acted on impulse and I forgot that we didn't even know each other that well. You had every right to be annoyed."

Oliver exhaled loudly and placed his hands behind him. "I had had a bad day. I lost one of my friends to a heart attack, and when I arrived at the clinic, Sam was crying because people were misjudging her and because she couldn't help her patient. It was so many things at once. I'm sorry too. I took my frustration out on you because you took your frustration out on me."

"That makes sense," Leticia said. "We took our frustrations out on each other. So, we're even now."

Oliver chuckled. "How's your finger?"

"It's all healed."

"That's good to know."

Leticia felt the awkward silence settle in, but she had one way to salvage the nice conversation she was having with a nice man.

"I have a question, Doctor Randall," Leticia said. "If you don't mind."

"Ask away."

"What do you think causes repetitive dreams?" she asked.

"Repetitive dreams?"

"Like, when you have the same dream almost every night. It starts off as a nice dream but then turns into a nightmare. The details hardly change."

Oliver stopped to think. "I'm not quite sure, but... what's the dream about?"

Leticia rubbed her hand over her forehead. Oliver was still a stranger and she wasn't comfortable telling him about Dwight.

"It's all right," Oliver said, reading her facial expression. "You don't have to tell me. Do you think of the person or thing in your dreams frequently?"

"Well, from time to time."

"Do you think of it right before you go to bed? Like you think of it and hope that it doesn't appear in your dreams?"

"I always pray that it doesn't appear in my dreams."

"Then that might be the reason for the repetition. You keep thinking about it, so you dream about it. The more vividly you worry or see the contents of your dream, in reality, the more your mind paints the picture and plays it out while you sleep."

Leticia tilted her head to the side. It made sense in a way. Back in Minnesota when she didn't dream of Dwight, Leticia didn't think much of him either. They had problems to deal with and she was sometimes too tired to even think. Oliver had a point.

"But when I try not to think about something, I always think about it," Leticia said. "I don't know if that makes sense to you."

"It does."

"So, what do I do then?"

"Occupy your mind with something else. Let something in your present fill that gap. It might take a while, but your brain will forget."

Leticia bowed her head, thinking of Oliver's words. Now that Carolyn and Margaret were soon to start new lives, she was going to have even more time on her hands. More time to think about Dwight. What in the world was going to fill that void?

"Would you like to dance, Leticia?" Oliver asked, catching her by surprise.

Leticia gulped. "What? Dance?"

Those eyes were dangerous. He just told her to occupy her mind with something else, yet here he was, with Dwight's eyes, asking her to dance with him.

"Yes," Oliver said. "Will you share this dance with me?"

"Of course," Leticia said.

There was no reasonable explanation as to why she had said yes that easily. She had turned so many men down and here she was being led to the dance floor.

Oliver held her gently and she felt safe in his arms. She liked the sound of his voice, how gentle he was for someone with such big hands. How was she supposed to say no to him with that smile he had?

"So, would you like me to help you with this dream of yours?" Oliver asked. "I might not know much about it, but I could read up on the subject and help you to the best of my ability. Take it as my apology for that incident."

"Yes, please," Leticia said softly.

Leticia searched the room for her friends with her eyes. They were standing at different corners, wrapped in the arms of the men they loved. They were all heading down different paths from that point, but Leticia was sure that they were never going to lose each other.

CHAPTER TWENTY-SEVEN

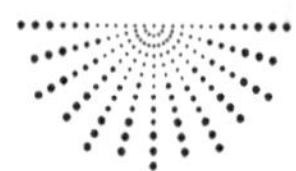

Deep in the forest, some miles from South Dakota, a raggedy-looking man with an unkempt beard stood over a dying fire. He poured his coffee in it, nearly putting out the flames. It was difficult staying warm during the night, especially in the forest.

Another man, who seemed to care a lot about his appearance sat on the ground with a newspaper clipping in his hand. His blond hair had grown an inch in the last month, and his beard had started to itch him. He read the heading of the clipping, smirked, and stretched, passing it to the man standing by the fire.

"Check this out," he said, handing the paper over.

The raggedy-looking man took the paper from him and with his croaky voice, he read the first line out loud.

"Appleton, South Dakota, celebrates their new town preacher, Sherman Johnstone."

The man scoffed and squeezed the paper, angrily stuffing it into the satchel. "Hmm. Our friend is quite popular now."

The man with blond hair laughed. "It'll make things even more interesting, don't you think, Porter?"

"I'll crush them, Brandon. They ruined me."

"By the way, how long do we have to keep going before we reach where we're headed?"

Porter walked over to the man and sat. "I have an idea. But we'll find out soon enough. It's morning, so we are bound to run into a few people. We could just ask them."

Porter laid on his back and stared into space. It had slowly turned into an obsession. This thing he was chasing. Porter had returned to Minnesota after his last encounter with Sherman in the forest but he couldn't concentrate on anything. No one had ever disrespected him that way. He would have let it go, if it wasn't for the fact that the town found out about how the nurses had double-crossed him, thereby, ruining business for them.

"Porter, do you have a plan?" Brandon asked him.

"I haven't thought of one," Porter said. "Right now, our focus is on finding them. When we do, we will figure out what we want to do."

Brandon's motive was unclear to Porter. The man was not obsessed with revenge, he was obsessed with the nurse called Carolyn. He might not admit it, but Porter knew that was the case. She was the one that got away.

"Do you have a plan, Brandon?"

"Revenge, of course. How? I'm not so sure."

"We should be on our way," Porter said, rising to his feet. "We have a long journey ahead of us. We need to get supplies too. I think we should stop in the next town we see and get food, water, and coffee."

"No, Porter," Brandon protested. "We can rely on the little we have for now until we reach Appleton."

"Are you a fool?" Porter rasped. "We barely have enough to get by today."

"If we go into town, someone might recognize us, and inform Sherman that we're coming."

Porter clenched his jaw. Sometimes, he wondered why he put up with a daft man like Brandon. They didn't think alike.

"We aren't even close to Appleton," Porter rasped. "And we are far from Minnesota, who is going to recognize us?"

"We can't take that risk."

"What risk? What is wrong with you? Should we starve then because you don't want to be seen?"

"I am not the one that poured the last of the coffee, to put out a fire? And still didn't."

"Brandon, I swear I will break your jaw," Porter threatened. "We are stopping at the next town and getting food. I advise you to tame your stupidity and speak to me with a clear head because you are getting on my nerves, and I might just unleash the pent-up frustration I have for our enemies... on you."

Brandon took a step back. "All right, fine. You're right, we are still a bit far from Appleton. We can stop. But we need to figure out just how far away we are, what town is the next town, and all of that. So we don't make any mistakes. This is supposed to be a surprise attack, remember?"

Just as Brandon finished his sentence, a wagon ambled down the path, in their direction. A family, consisting of a father, a mother, and two teenagers sat in it. Porter stood on the side and waved at them to slow down.

"Good morning, good folks," he greeted, feigning a friendly smile.

"Good morning," the man answered. "How can we help you?"

"I was wondering if you know of the town called Appleton," Porter asked.

"I do, we get fresh produce from them every quarter," the man said.

"Excellent. Would you happen to know how long it might take us to reach Appleton?"

"You are far off from there, I'm afraid. That's several days of travel," he answered. "Maybe a week on foot. Maybe more. But you're headed in the right direction."

"Ah." Porter nodded. "And where might the closest town be? If I may ask."

"Let me think," the man said. "Oh, that would be Cutter's Ridge. It's only a few hours that way. You can't miss it. It's a small town though, so don't expect much."

"Thank you so much," Porter said. "You are a good man."

Porter stepped aside to let the wagon pass. He knew that they were several days away from Appleton, but he just had to ask so that Brandon would rest assured. Another thing Brandon was obsessed with was the element of surprise. He didn't want Sherman or the nurses to know of their arrival. Porter, on the other hand, couldn't care less. As long as he got his revenge, he was totally fine with them anticipating his coming or not.

"So, we go to Cutter's Ridge and get food," Porter said. "It's fine if you don't want to come. I'll go alone and get food for myself."

"No, I'll come. We're still very far from Appleton anyway. Do you think we need better weapons?" Brandon asked as they continued down the path. "We might need ropes, guns, knives..."

"We'll get them. Or we make do with the ones we have," Porter said. "Right now, our main focus is getting to Appleton as soon as we can."

"I thought food was our main focus right now."

"It is," Porter said through clenched teeth. "And, let me ask you this, Brandon. I should have asked before we left Minnesota, but I forgot. Do you really want revenge, or do you just want Carolyn?"

"Both," Brandon said. "I want what you want, Porter, never doubt that for a second. I want to destroy the people who humiliated us. The preacher with his ego, Carolyn, who had the audacity to betray me, and her friend who pointed a gun at me. Every one of them will pay for the humiliation they caused us. We can't go back to Minnesota because of it. Because people laugh at us. They say a group of frail women were able to take us down. Able to ruin our business. They are not getting away with it. We will make sure of it."

Porter smiled. Brandon took the words right out of his mouth. "Now, I want you to focus on that energy and never let it die. Because you will need it when we face them. They will pretend to be innocent, but they are not. They are backstabbers who bit the hand that fed them. The hand that was providing for them. They poisoned the minds of my girls and turned them against me. For that, they will pay. They will pay, even if they do so with their blood."

The faces of Sherman, Carolyn Darby, Margaret Sampson, and Leticia Baker were the last things Porter saw before he went to bed and the first things he saw when he woke up. They had become his drive, the push he needed to get payback. It took Porter months to find them, he paid people a lot of money to trace them and when he finally got them in a precise location, he left his home and never looked back.

With only revenge on their minds, Porter Hathaway and Brandon Eckert made their way to South Dakota. They glanced at each other and exchanged sinister laughs. They were coming for what was rightfully theirs and no man alive was going to stop them.

If you enjoyed this book then you can grab Leticia's Story – The Grieving Bride here, or read on for a preview.

LETICIA - THE GRIEVING BRIDE - PREVIEW

Leticia rubbed her palms together and blew into them for warmth. It had rained the night before, the air was chilly and the path was muddy. There was a soft squishing sound with every step she took. Looking down, she was regretting wearing her nice pair of white shoes to visit the town.

Leticia hated wearing shoes except when necessary, but Margaret had said that they looked good on her. It was silly, but she wanted to look good. However, due to the rain, they were stained with mud, even the pretty bow on the top.

Leticia exhaled and looked up at the sky. It was bright out that morning, but the sun was hiding behind clouds and not that warm.

"The perfect weather for a stroll around town," she said with a sigh. "If only my shoes weren't ruined."

Carolyn and Margaret were starting to notice the change in her demeanor. Gently teasing her because she was dressing differently, her hair was neat all of the time, and she wore shoes more than she usually did, especially to town. They guessed that she had grown bored since they were always with their beaus. Leticia let them believe that, but she knew they were completely wrong.

To get to town, she had to pass the local doctors who ran a clinic from his house. A week ago, she had run into Oliver, the doctor in front of his house. It had been completely coincidental, but she noticed that her heart skipped a beat when she laid eyes on him. Her normal response to things she could not explain was to ignore them, but this time, she decided not to. So, to confirm just how much effect Oliver had on her, Leticia tried to run into him again. It took three days, but she successfully bumped into him on the road. To her surprise, not only did her heart skip a beat, but she was sure that she felt butterflies in her stomach when he smiled at her.

It all started at the dance. At least, that was as far back as Leticia could trace the change in her feeling.

Two weeks ago, she had apologized to Oliver for slapping him across the face and misjudging him. Oliver had accepted her apology and had even asked her to a dance. During the night, they danced twice, and their conversations were light and filled with laughter. Oliver was always quick to offer his help, and somehow, Leticia had managed to look past the fact that the local doctor reminded her so much of the man she once loved. The conversations she had with Oliver had convinced her that he and Dwight were two completely different people. Apart from the fact that they had the same exact eyes, they were nothing alike.

Oliver seemed warmer. Obviously kind. Leticia liked those traits about him. It was the first time in a long time that she had been curious about somebody. In the last two weeks, she had met Oliver five times and she recalled everything about their encounters. A chuckle escaped her as she remembered how her cheeks hurt because she couldn't stop smiling, how she replayed their conversations at every chance she got, how Carolyn and Margaret were starting to suspect her, and how she was always looking forward to seeing him again.

Leticia had convinced herself that Oliver liked her too. Not just as a friend that he was helping with her trauma, but as a woman. That's what she wanted to believe. It made the scenarios in her head romantic. Leticia had told him about her dreams and Oliver had recommended some soothing herbs for her to take before bed. He made sure to ask her about it every time they met.

Was she reading too much into it? How she hoped not, for she felt her heart could be broken once more if the doctor rejected her.

"Leticia, it's so nice to see you today."

There was only one person with that voice and hearing it sent tingles down her spine. Leticia smiled and tucked the loose strands of her blonde hair behind her ear as she turned around slowly. It had been three days since she had last seen Oliver and she sighed in relief, thankful that she had decided to take her walk today.

"Good morning, Doctor Randall," Leticia beamed. "A beautiful morning, isn't it? She lowered her eyes for the handsome and broad-shouldered man always took her breath away. Despite the grey in his hair, he had a face that drew her glance and icy blue eyes that still reminded her of Dwight.

"It is indeed," he answered, placing his arms behind his back. "I see you're on your way to town."

Leticia glanced at the basket in her hand. "I am. It's for Edwin."

Oliver gestured for them to keep walking. He stayed by her side, keeping his arms behind him as they strolled down the path. "Edwin?" he asked. "Is he all right?"

"Oh, he's fine. I am buying foodstuffs for a dinner we're hosting in a couple of days. Edwin wishes to marry Margaret. We're celebrating it, so Carolyn and I are setting everything up and getting things ready."

"A party? That's wonderful. I'm sure Margaret's thrilled by the news."

"She doesn't know," Leticia answered. "Edwin came to Carolyn and me in secret."

"Ah," Oliver said softly. "I'd love to see her reaction to his proposal."

"You can," Leticia said without sparing a minute to think about it. "I'd like to invite you to the dinner. Please. I'd be glad if you came."

Oliver smiled. "Absolutely. I'll be there."

It felt like Leticia had achieved a great feat. Inviting Oliver to dinner was a big step for her, and seeing how desperate she had been for him to say yes, it confirmed how much she had grown to like him. It made sense that she thought about him all of the time.

Leticia slowed her pace and walked two steps behind Oliver. She watched him, secretly admiring his features. Thankfully, his eyes didn't affect her as much as they used to. The silver-tone in his brown hair seemed to have increased. Oliver liked to keep his hair out of his face. He maintained his ducktail haircut, and his face was neatly shaved.

She had asked around about Oliver from some of the townsfolk, and they had nothing but good things to say about him. Oliver was in his early forties, he loved the church, loved his daughter, and was charitable. The mere thought that he might like her excited Leticia. If only there was a way to confirm it.

"Is it weird that I cannot seem to get our dance off my mind?" Oliver asked.

"What?" Leticia blurted out and turned to him. *Did that mean?*

Read Leticia -The Grieving Bride here

FROM BRAVE NURSES TO
Courageous Brides
Leticia
THE GRIEVING BRIDE

The Brides of Broken Bow

If you missed any of this series, all three books are now available.
Each book covers one couple and is a complete story.

God bless,

Indiana Wake

Indiana Wake was born in Denver, Colorado, where she learned to love the outdoors and horses. At the age of eleven, her parents moved to the United Kingdom to follow her father's career.

It was a strange and foreign new world, and it took a while for her to settle down. Her mom raised horses and Indiana soon learned to ride. She would often escape on horseback imagining she was back in the Wild West. As well as horses, Indiana escaped into fiction and dreamed of all the friends she had left behind.

From an early age, she loved stories. They were always sweet and clean and, more often than not, included horses, cowboys and most importantly of all a happy ever after. As she got older, she would often be found making up her own stories and would tell them to anyone who would listen.

As she grew up, she continued to write, but marriage and a job stole some of her dreams. Then one day she was discussing with a friend at church, how hard it was to get sweet and clean fiction. Though very shy about her writing Indiana agreed to share one of her stories. That friend loved the story and suggested she publish it on kindle. Together they worked really hard, and the rest, as they say, is history.

Indiana has had multiple number one bestsellers and now makes her living from her writing. She believes she was truly blessed to be given this opportunity and thanks each and every one of her readers for making her dream come true.